WHITE
GRIZZLY

Mary Peace Finley

WHITE GRIZZLY

FILTER PRESS, LLC
Palmer Lake, Colorado

To the students of Vicki Fuesz in Sterling, Colorado, who inspired me to write again. This book is for you.

Library of Congress Cataloging-in-Publication Data

Finley, Mary Peace.
   White grizzly / Mary Peace Finley.
      p. cm.
   Summary: In 1845, when he leaves the Cheyenne village where he has been living and sets out from Bent's Fort along the Sante Fe Trail in search of his white grandfather, Julio faces danger from renegade Texans, the Pawnee Indians, and a grizzly bear, before finding where he truly belongs.
   ISBN 0-86541-058-5 (paperback)
   [1. Identity--Fiction. 2. Frontier and pioneer life--West (U.S.)--Fiction. 3. West (U.S.)--Fiction.] I. Title.

PZ7.F4962 Wh 2000
[Fic]--dc21

                                          00-037581

Filter Press, LLC
P.O. Box 95
Palmer Lake, Colorado 80133

Manufactured in the United States of America

Acknowledgments

I am grateful for the expertise and joyful wisdom of my editor, Connie Epstein; for advice on dog behavior from Randy Pritchard, D.V.M.; for consultation on sheep and sheepherding from Myrtle and Roy Dow of Black Pine Sheep Ranch, Colorado; for help with French words and phrases from Virginia Fox; for advice on Spanish words and phrases from Olgy Gary; for proofreading, Janie Crisp; and for gently herding the team down the trail, wagon master Doris Baker.

Special thanks to my beloved husband, Wally Finley, for patiently listening to many revisions, and to my writer-friend Lou Dean Jacobs for her searing critiques and impassioned support.

PIKES PEAK

Arkansas River

BENT'S FORT   GRIZZLY ATTACK

BIG TIMBERS

POINT OF ROCK

SPANISH PEAKS

Sangre de Cristo Mountains

SANTA FE TRAIL

Rio de las Animas Perdidas en Purgatorio

CIMARRON ROUTE—SANTA FE TRAIL

Cimarron River

THE SMITH BROTHERS JOIN THE WAGON TRAIN

N. Canadian River

TAOS

SANTA FE

Pecos River

Canadian River

---JULIO'S ROUTE
——SANTA FE TRAIL

1

Julio stopped at the crest of a sand hill and stared. Below, Bent's Fort rose from the prairie, tall and solid as rock, two stories high with double gates opened wide as if in welcome. He dropped to his knees, swung the basket off his back, and let it tumble onto the sand. "Someone in there has to know, Chivita."

With an excited "Eerp!" Chivita leaped into Julio's arms, a bundle of black and white, nuzzling his chin and ears with her nose. "That's it, Chivita!" Julio ducked away from her tickling tongue. "Clean me up. Make me look good before we go inside."

Chivita backed away and cocked her head, one brow raised.

Julio glanced down at his bare chest, the ragged pantalones, pants that were new and white when he and Papá left Taos, and at the beaded Cheyenne moccasins on his feet. "You're right. Impossible." He stood, brushing away strands of sun-bleached hair that dangled like yellow straw in front of his eyes. He slipped his reed flute into the leather bag at his side, straightened the shoulder strap, and wiggled the woven basket into place on his back. "Vamos, Chivita. Let's go."

After three days alone since he had parted company with the Cheyenne, the noise from Bent's Fort thundered against his ears. It looked as if the whole world had come here to trade—or to join the eastbound spring caravan. A line of wagons stretched for half a mile, waiting to be hitched to mules or oxen or horses. Beneath a large United States flag that slapped against a pole above the second floor, people rushed back and forth between the Fort and the wagons.

Julio sprinted toward the gates, but slowed and traced the sign of the cross over his forehead and chest as he passed a mound of freshly turned dirt where a wooden cross marked a new grave. He couldn't read the words on the marker, but the date was the same as the date he'd carved less than two months ago on the aspen tree near Papá's lonely grave in the mountains—1845. A gunshot jolted him from the memory of digging with Papá's shiny new coffeepot and his own bare hands.

Men cheered. The impact of pounding hoofs vibrated through his moccasins, and he tasted dust billowing from beneath the surface layer of mud that remained after the days of rain. Through an opening between wagons, he spotted an oval racetrack to the north of the thick Fort walls. "It's just a horse race, Chivita. Not an attack."

Trampled grass and wagon ruts narrowed as the toes of his moccasins nosed toward the gates. He hopped over the tongue of a wagon, and his hand reached out to the studded metal that clad the enormous gate. The metal was cold to his touch, almost sharp.

"Hola." He called out. "Hello?"

A man gave him a strange look, but didn't answer.

"Vamos, Chivita," Julio whispered, patting his leg, and eased into the cool, dark entryway. He blinked in the sudden darkness, groping for the wall to guide him. A shiver went through him, not from the cool adobe bricks, but from touching walls Papá had made. Ay, Papá! he thought, I wish you were here.

"Hey! Watch where you're going!" Silhouetted black against the glaring light, a burly man balancing a huge square bundle on his shoulder barreled into the dark passageway, nearly knocking Julio down. "You can't go inside! Injuns trade here." The profile of the man's bearded chin pointed toward the entryway wall. "At that window." The man swaggered on.

"What do you have?" A dim face appeared at the small opening in the thick adobe wall.

Julio backed away. "Nothing."

"Then git on back outside."

"I don't have anything to trade." Julio stepped up to the window. "I came to see Mr. Bent."

"Tarnation!" the voice exclaimed. "Hey, Red!" the man called over his shoulder. "This feller speaks English better than you do!"

"What does he want?"

"Says he wants to see William."

Julio peered through the window into a room filled with trade goods, spotted the second man who was unloading a wooden box of clay pipes onto a shelf, and raised his voice so he would hear. "I have to talk with Mr. Bent."

The redheaded man set the pipes down. "I'll see what he wants. Come on in," he called to Julio.

Julio stepped from the passageway into a large courtyard. Sunshine beat down and reflected from the light colored dirt. Squinting as his eyes adjusted to the brightness, Julio focused on rows of doors. So many doors!

Doors all around the ground floor, doors off the second-floor catwalk, and wide passageways that led farther back off the courtyard. Bent's Fort was as big as all of Taos! From the wonderful aroma of roasting meat and boiling coffee, Julio knew someone was cooking behind one door back there, and his stomach rumbled. Through another doorway, he saw the glow of coals and heard the hiss of bellows and the clanging of a hammer against metal and, from another, the sound of a saw cutting wood.

The man with bright red hair and a nose covered with rusty red freckles and flaking white skin stepped from inside the trade room.

"Hello," Julio said.

The redhead frowned, looking him over from the tips of his moccasins to the top of his head. "Well, where did you come from?"

"From Taos. I need to talk with Mr. Bent."

Red chuckled lightly and shook his head. "Mr. Bent is a busy man. A very busy man, especially today."

"But I have to see him. He knows I'm coming."

Red's eyebrows knotted slightly. "Well, you can talk to me. What do you need?"

"I'm Julio Montoya." Julio watched Red's eyes, but there was no look of recognition. "Enrique's son." Still no look of understanding. "I'm Julio Montoya," he said again. "I'm the son of Enrique Montoya, the adobe maker from Taos."

"Enrique?" Red's eyebrows lurched, and once again he studied Julio from top to toe. The look on his face changed from disbelief to uncertainty. "You're Enrique's son?"

"Yes."

"Well, er, ummm." Red glanced toward the trade-room door, then over his shoulder toward the second floor, hesitating. "Well, I don't know," he said. "Follow me. I'll see."

Julio followed Red across the courtyard toward a split log stairway that led to the second-floor catwalk.

"Ven! Come!" Julio urged Chivita up the stairs, then followed Red toward a little house that looked to Julio like Mamá's tiny adobe casita in Taos, except it sat on a flat roof instead of on the ground beside a stream.

A few yards from the casita Red stopped. "Wait here," he said. He approached the door, paused, and cautiously stepped inside.

Julio listened, but hearing no voices, turned and looked out over the adobe wall that surrounded the second floor. This view was even better than if he had climbed high in a cottonwood tree. With no branches in the way, he could see the vast plains surrounding the Fort and the sheep grazing by the Nepesta, the river Americans call the Arkansas and Cheyenne call the Arrow Flint. Until yesterday, the tipis of the Cheyenne village had clustered there, each with its own fire circle. Now nothing was left of the village but pressed grass, dead coals, and discarded bones, as if a whole piece of his life had been sliced away. Across the western horizon, vast mountain ranges stretched as far as he could see north and south. "How did we ever make it through those mountains, Chivita?"

Chivita jumped up, front paws on his leg, but catapulted off barking at the sound of a loud, angry-sounding voice.

"—been expecting him for days! Bring him in!"

"Easy, Chivita." Julio gave the signal to quiet.

Red motioned to Julio from the door of the casita and stepped aside.

So this was William Bent! Julio had imagined the owner of Bent's Fort as a giant, but the man with dark hair and sunken eyes leaning over papers and writing at a small wooden table was not a big man at all. Julio rapped against the doorframe with his knuckles. "Pardon me, Mr. Bent. I'm sorry to interrupt, but I have to ask you a question."

William Bent looked up.

"I'm Julio Montoya. My papá, Enrique Montoya, helped you build this Fort. He was an adobe maker."

The pen dropped. Bent pushed the palms of his hands flat against the tabletop, slowly stood, then circled around Julio, turning him to face the light. "You're not Enrique's son." He squinted into Julio's eyes. "You can't be! With that yellow hair? And green eyes? Who put you up to this? Texans? Get him out of here, Red."

Red's hand tightened around Julio's arm. "What shall I do with him?"

"Just get him out of here. Send him back to wherever he came from." Bent waved his hand as if shooing a fly and sat down at his desk.

"I'm from Taos, Mr. Bent!" Julio struggled against Red. "And I *am* Julio Montoya! Enrique was my papá." He grabbed the doorframe. "Papá came home with your letter, and your brother Charles sent a message back to you."

Bent looked up, frowning. "A message?" he grumbled. "About what?"

"I-I don't know," Julio stammered. "Papá said it was about war. He said you were worried about what's going to happen."

"Any fool knows that," Bent said with a harrumph.

"After we left Taos, we—Papá and I—tried to catch up with the wagons, but the Jicarilla Apaches found us and . . . and. . . ." Julio pressed his eyes closed. Papá's death was too horrible to remember.

Julio heard Bent's chair scrape against the dirt floor, and Red's grip on his arm relaxed.

"Where's the message?" Bent stood before him with his hand extended.

"Ay, no!" Julio's knees went weak. "Didn't you get it? After Papá—after everything that happened—I sent the message to you with a sheepherder. Helacio was coming with a wagon train."

Julio saw Bent glance over his head and nod, and Red turned loose of Julio's arm. Bent's face softened. "Well, you sure don't look like you could be Enrique's son." He looked down at the floor and sighed. "I'm sorry about your father, Julio." He ran his hand over a stubble of beard. "Awful sorry. Here, sit down. You've had a long, hard journey." As Bent slumped back into his chair, Julio eased down onto the edge of a wooden stool.

"Julio, your father was a fine man, an honorable man. I couldn't have built this Fort without him." Bent leaned forward and began to sort through a stack of papers on his desk. At the sight of the torn message stained with Papá's blood, Julio's stomach lurched, and he looked away. "The sheepherder told me those confounded Apaches killed your papá," Bent said. "How did you escape? How did you get here?"

How could he possibly answer? So much had happened. "At first, alone. The Apaches took everything, even Chivita. I came on, but I lost the trail in a snowstorm.

Chivita found me. I was sick. We were both starving, and I was snow-blind." He reached down to touch Chivita. "Then the Cheyenne helped us. But I had to get here, Mr. Bent. I had to see you. There's something I have to know."

"Well, I know one thing for sure." Bent shook his head. "You're lucky you made it. Lucky you escaped the Apaches, lucky Texas freebooters didn't find you and toss your body to the wolves. Your papá would be proud of you. Very proud." Bent ran his hand across his chin, and for a moment his thoughts seemed far away. Then abruptly he looked up. "How old are you anyway?"

"I don't know," Julio said. "Thirteen, maybe fourteen. But that's what I want to know! I want to know when I was born. And where!" Julio took in a long, deep breath. For as long as he could remember, this was the moment he'd been waiting for. Fighting to control his voice, he began again. "I've always looked different from the rest of my family—this hair, this light skin. Just before Papá died, he told me why."

Julio looked from Bent to Red and back again.

"Papá said he found me near a burned-out wagon along the Purgatory River. I was the only one left alive." Squaring his shoulders, Julio looked straight into Bent's deep-set eyes. "Who were those people, Mr. Bent? Where did they come from? Papá said someone here at Bent's Fort knows. Did he tell you, Mr. Bent? Do you know who I am?"

2

"I'm afraid I don't, Julio." Bent shrugged. "I know your papá was proud of you. But until today I didn't know you weren't his own son. He was a private man, quiet."

The horse races were over. Julio stood beside Bent on the catwalk, watching the crowd of men jostling into the courtyard below. Some were fanning fistfuls of money, strutting and screeching like the peacock on the catwalk. Bent waved his hand over the boisterous crowd. "He could have told any of those men down there about you. Come this way."

Julio followed Bent inside and down a stairway into a large room with tables spread with white cloths. Instead of crossing the room, Bent doubled back through a doorway into another room. An American-style bed covered with a bright colored quilt stood near a large kitchen. That was where the wonderful smells were coming from. Above the bed hung a plain wooden cross.

"Mr. Bent, where's the priest?"

Bent looked as if he'd caught a whiff of spoiled food. "Priest?"

"The priest here at the Fort."

"There's no priest at this Fort, Julio." A smile tugged at the corner of Bent's lip. "And there never will be! Closest priest's that rascal Martinez in Taos." Abruptly he straightened. "Oh." The look on his face changed, and so did his voice. "For your father?"

Julio nodded. "Papá wasn't blessed by a priest before he died. I don't want his soul trapped in purgatory."

"Look, Julio." Bent exhaled deeply as he leaned one hand on the underside of the stairs. "For what it's worth, seems to me that if a man's a good man like Enrique was, then whatever waits for him after he dies—God, Dios, Great Spirit—whatever it is will know he was a good man without being told by some priest, Catholic or otherwise."

Julio stared into the dark area beneath the stairs, then his focus wandered to the colors of the brightly patterned quilt across the room. Was purgatory something only people in Taos believed in, or only Catholics believed? "Are you Catholic, Mr. Bent?"

Air hissed through Bent's nostrils. "No."

"Then do you believe the Cheyenne way?"

"Hey!" A woman's loud voice suddenly boomed from the kitchen. "Hey, you! Get outa' here! Go on! Git!" Chivita tore through the doorway, and Julio tackled her as she skidded by.

"Chivita! Stay, Chivita." Chivita wriggled in his arms.

"Chivita?" Bent laughed. "You call that little dog *chivita,* little goat?"

Julio nodded. "Papá suckled her to a goat so she'd be gentle with sheep. That's why we named her Chivita. She's the best sheep dog in Taos."

"Well, you'd better keep that little goat away from Charlotte." Bent nodded toward the kitchen. "She wouldn't take kindly to your dog stealing our dinner . . . and neither would I!" Bent stepped away from the stairs and pointed across the courtyard to a doorway in the southeast corner.

"Unload your gear over there in the workers' quarters. Then ask around. See what you can find out. Come back when Charlotte rings the dinner gong."

"Mr. Bent. I have to stay at the Fort until I find the man who talked with Papá." Julio held his hands out, palms open. "I don't have money to pay you, but my hands work hard. I'll mix adobe, make bricks. I'll earn my way. I always thought I'd be here making adobes with Papá, though, not alone."

"You want to work? That's good. Freeloaders don't get far with me." Bent rocked back on the heels of his boots and gestured in a wide circle. "But Julio, the Fort's finished. We don't need more adobes."

"You don't need adobes?"

"No," Bent said, shaking his head.

Two dreams, being here at Bent's Fort with Papá and making adobes, both shattered.

With the toe of his moccasin, Julio nudged the crumbling edge of a wall. "Do—do you have some little jobs for me to do until the next wagons head back to Taos?" Julio could scarcely believe the words that came from his mouth. Little jobs? Little jobs! I didn't come all this way for little jobs! And I can't go back to Taos until I find out the rest of what Papá was telling me. The leather sole of his moccasin crushed the crumbling adobe against the floor. "Adobe always needs repair," he heard himself say. "Especially after rain. It's rained a lot in the past week."

Bent nodded and patted Julio's shoulder, a pat that was a push out the door.

Julio crossed the courtyard, weaving his way through groups of men still excited about the race. Papá would have talked with the priest—if there had been one—but these men didn't seem like the kind he would have confided in.

"Eh, don't be such a sorry loser!" A shaggy-looking trapper punched another man's sagging shoulder, and Julio sidestepped out of the way. "Likely you'll win it back off'a me 'fore the moon sets anyhows."

The second man caught his balance and snatched two decks of cards from beneath the leather fringes of his clothes. He slapped the cards down on a stack of dusty buffalo hides beside the fur press in the middle of the courtyard. "Poker or monte?" he challenged.

"Monte," the trapper said. "Loser deals."

Julio edged toward them. "Do—did either of you know Enrique Montoya?"

"Never heard of 'em." Without looking up, the loser slapped a card onto the hides.

There were people everywhere. How could he ask them all?

A young American trader stood in a semicircle of onlookers, flipping a wooden ball above his hand, then trying to catch it in a small wooden cup that was attached to the ball by a string. Julio dodged his way past pointed elbows, repeating to one man after another. "Did you know Enrique Montoya, an adobe maker from Taos? Did you know Enrique Montoya? Do you remember a Mexican man who worked here for three years, Enrique Montoya?"

"Enrique?" The ball clicked onto the post with a sturdy whack. The trader smiled. "The 'dobe maker?"

"Yes!" Julio's breath caught in his throat. "Did you know him? Did you ever talk with him?"

"Well, yes, but nothing much more than 'hola' or 'buenos dias'."

Julio sighed. "Did any of you?"

"Don't think so," someone replied, reaching for the cup and ball. "Let me try that."

Julio walked on through the courtyard. Other men strolled by, talking and smoking cigarettes. Julio studied each man's face. Who? Who would know? People came and went from the Fort every day, he realized. Maybe the man Papá talked to had already gone. Papá started for Taos six or eight weeks ago, so it had been a long time.

On the opposite side of the courtyard, Julio entered a dusky hall. There were no windows; the only light came in through the door. Other doors opened off each side of the hall, one to the right, one to the left. Julio stepped into the room on his left. Hats, ropes, and clothes hung from pegs on the walls. Rolled sleeping mats rested against the walls along the edges of the floor. In spite of the heat outside, a low fire burned in the corner fireplace, simmering beans in an iron pot and filling the room with the smells of charcoal and home. Julio's mouth watered. He hadn't tasted beans and tortillas since the first day on the trail with Papá.

From the room across the hall, Julio heard the slap-slap-slap of hands patting out tortillas. That sound! It was almost the same rhythm as his sister Teresita's when she made tortillas. Suddenly he was overwhelmed with a longing for familiar hands. When Mamá made tortillas, her pats were slow and sharp as if she were angry. Teresita's were faster, lighter, like the wings of a fluttering dove. He could tell each of his sisters by her own way of patting out tortillas.

Julio swung the basket off his shoulder and propped it against a wall. Papá's things were on top of the load. He lifted the bundle to his face and drew in a long breath through the scratchy wool, but Papá's smell was gone.

"Ven, Chivita. Come." He hugged the bundle to his chest, walked outside, and sank onto a log bench. Taking Chivita's head in his hands, he leaned back against the hot adobe wall, Papá's adobe wall. The sun was shining at an angle now, casting long shadows. The pace of the day was slowing down. More men had joined the game of monte, tossing brightly colored cards and shiny coins onto the buffalo hide. Papá would have talked with someone from Taos, he thought, another Mexican, not an American.

A bronze-skinned woman with high cheekbones came through the doorway beside him, carrying a tin bowl of beans and tortillas still steaming from the *comál*. *"Tienes hambre, joven?* Are you hungry, young man?"

"Gracias, Señora." Julio took the bowl gingerly. The tin was so hot he quickly set it on the bench. Hands trembling, Julio dipped the tortilla into the beans. When he looked up, the woman was still there, leaning against the doorpost.

"You must be starved," she said in Spanish. "I'll bring more."

"Can you give my dog something too?"

When the woman returned with a meaty bone, her eyes were red. "I'm sorry about your papá," she said softly. *"Qué Dios le bendiga.* May God bless his soul."

Beans slid from Julio's tortilla and dropped back into the bowl. "Did you know Papá?"

"Sí. We were friends. Enrique was *un buen hombre*, a good man."

"How did you know he's my papá?"

The woman brushed her hair away from her forehead with the back of her hand and smiled slightly. "Sometimes this big Fort is a very small place. News travels like prairie fire. So do secrets."

"Secrets?" Julio said, watching carefully for her reaction. "Did—did Papá tell you a secret . . . about me?"

The woman's eyebrows raised. She shook her head, then looking up, pointed with her chin toward another woman wearing a long American-style calico dress with big sleeves and a full skirt covered by a billowing white apron. She was coming through the doorway at the far side of the courtyard where Julio had been with Mr. Bent. "I cook for the workers. Charlotte there, she cooks for los Americanos. *Mire.* Watch."

Charlotte held a metal triangle in front of her and clanged it with a metal rod. Immediately the monte game ended. Men jostled each other as they funneled into two streams, one stream heading toward the big dining room, the other toward Julio and the workers' quarters.

Candles and lanterns flickered through the dining-room windows. Julio saw Mr. Bent and several other Americans sitting down at the tables covered with white cloths.

Julio picked up the bundle of Papá's things, stood, and walked toward the open door.

"Ay, no!" The woman grabbed his arm. "You can't go in there! That's for los Americanos. You eat here with the workers."

"Mr. Bent invited me." Julio tugged a lock of his hair. "Maybe that was Papá's secret," he said. "Maybe I'm one of them—un Americano."

3

"Yes! The government! Missouri's the richest state in the Union because of trade with Mexico. All that Mexican silver and gold, and our government is talking war? It just doesn't make sense!"

Julio waited for a break in the heated discussion.

"Ask me, it's all on account of 'em Texans and that confounded bankrupt Republic of theirs. Republic—huh! They's probably some of 'em settlers 'ats good folk, but they's plenty 'at ain't settling, and they's plenty 'at ain't no good a'tall! Like them freebooters 'at killed that fellow, Chávez."

"And attacked that village—what was it called?"

"Mora," Julio said without thinking.

"Yup, Moor!"

"Oh, Julio! There you are. Come in." Bent stood and pulled a stool to his side. "Sit down. Eat."

Charlotte and a white woman wearing an apron carried steaming bowls and platters to the table. One platter was piled high with roasted buffalo hump. Even after two bowls of beans, he was still hungry.

Julio watched the men eating American style with forks and sipping red wine from glass cups that looked like poppies on long stems. His sister, Teresita, had told him about the strange ways people ate in Charles Bent's

home in Taos where she worked. Here, people ate the same
way. Awkwardly he picked up a three-pronged fork, trying
to balance it on his fingers.

"Mr. Bent, I asked people in the courtyard about Papá.
Nobody knew. Could I ask these men while they're eating?"
Bent shrugged, nodded. "Lend an ear, fellas." His voice
rose. "You've all heard what happened to Enrique. Well,
this is Enrique's son, Julio. He's trying to find out
something about his past."

In spite of the discomfort of so many eyes looking at
him, Julio began. "Just before Papá died, he told how he
found me." The men listened while they chewed,
occasionally glancing up from their plates when Charlotte
and the other woman set more platters of food before them.
"He and his compañeros found a burned-out wagon on the
Purgatory—el Río de las Animas Perdidas en Purgatorio,
the River of Souls Lost in Purgatory. Is that somewhere
near here?"

"The Purgatory joins the Arkansas about ten miles
downriver," Bent answered.

"Well, Papá and his friends found a man and woman
and little girl there. They were dead. A boy was the only
one left alive." Julio searched one face then another,
expecting to see a response, a memory, but there was none.
"That boy was me. I want to find out about those people.
Papá said someone here at Bent's Fort may know." He
finished by adding, "Did Papá tell any of you about me?
Or the wagon? Or anything?"

Not a single man answered. Julio stood, arms hanging
at his sides, with nothing more to say.

"Thank you, anyway," Julio said softly. He scooped
up his bundle and turned back toward the workers'

quarters, but stopped when he heard a loud voice coming from the kitchen.

"No, we cain't wait, Dick! We gotta tell the boy. Right now!" Charlotte shuffled into the dining room, tugging the arm of a man as dark as she was.

"Sorry, Mr. Bent," the man said, dabbing his moist face and strong neck with a bandanna. "I reckon we should have waited until you was finished eatin'." He shrugged. "But you know Charlotte!"

Bent laughed. "Julio, meet Dick and Charlotte Green. Dick and Charlotte came here with me from Missouri. Dick's our smithy. Charlotte cooks for us."

Dick Green looked down at Julio, eyes filled with tenderness, and reached out with the largest, most muscle-bound hand Julio had ever seen. Then, as if suddenly remembering something almost forgotten, Dick Green straightened and pulled his hand away. "Charlotte and me, we're real sorry about your daddy, Mr. Julio. We was good friends, and—"

"We couldn't help from hearin' what you was jes' tellin' these men," Charlotte interrupted. "Your daddy tol' Dick that same story 'bout that man and woman in a wagon. White folks with two chillens, a girl and a towhead boy." She tugged a lock of Julio's blond hair. "And the boy was only one left alive, poor li'l thing. Ain't that what Enrique tol' you, Dick?"

"Yessum." Dick nodded. "Found that little one in July, Enrique said. That's why he named you Julio, 'cuz in Spanish that says July."

The inside of Julio's chest stretched with too much air. His hands trembled, and his knees suddenly turned so weak that he sat back down on the stool. His thoughts spun like crazed hornets. Dick must be the man Papá talked to.

The men scraped their benches and stools, stood and sauntered back outside, coughing and laughing, returning to card games and cigarettes. A harmonica tune wheezed, and from the catwalk the peacock screeched.

Julio waited until all the men had filed out before he tried to speak again. "Can you tell me anything else?"

"After Enrique tol' me about findin' you," Dick said, nodding, "I tol' mah wife here and—"

"I remembered that ol' gentleman in Independence. You remember him, Mr. Bent. The ol' gentleman with the store where you bought supplies 'fore we came. The place with gold letterin' on the window. Me and Dick must've gone there a hundred times, fetchin' flour and molasses and rice and calico and gunpowder."

"You mean Myron Forester?" Bent frowned.

"That's him! Forester's Mercantile."

Bent pivoted toward Julio and sat knee to knee, looking at him as if for the very first time. His eyes narrowed as he studied Julio's hair, then his face, then his bare chest. "Chance in a million," he said, shaking his head.

"What chance?" Julio's heart was flopping like a fish out of water. "Who is Myron Forester?"

"Like I said, Mr. Forester owns the store that outfitted us. Me and Dick was there so much, we got to know him. He's a widow man. He tol' us about his son travelin' west with a family—wife and two chillen—a boy and a girl. They disappeared."

"Eight, nine years ago, it was then," Dick said. "Mr. Forester said he was too old to go searchin' all the way from Missouri to the California Territory. The West was jus' too big, he said, so he opened a business to keep him in touch with folks headin' west. He's been askin' ever'body to watch for his family ever since. Said he'd wait ten years."

Dick lowered himself down onto one knee beside Julio. His huge hand reached out and rested warm on Julio's shoulder. "Your daddy, when I tol' him about Mr. Forester, he got real quiet. Finally he said, 'Julio should know about this. Soon.'"

A chill raced up Julio's spine. "So is Mr. Forester my grandfather?"

A smile spread from one side of Dick's face to the other, and his eyes brimmed with tears. "Shore looks to me like he is, Mr. Julio. Shore looks to me like he is."

Abruptly Mr. Bent scuffed his chair against the floor, pushing away from the table, and he began to pace around the room. "Now wait a minute here. Don't go jumping to conclusions, giving the boy false hopes. Enrique may have seen the similarity with Myron's story, but it doesn't mean there's any connection at all. People are lost all the time. It was nine or ten years ago!"

Bent fixed his gaze on Julio, running his fingers over the stubble on his chin. "And even if you were related to Myron, you don't know anything about his kind of life. Myron's a gentleman, an educated man. After the way you've lived, that life wouldn't suit you at all—proper dress, proper speech, teacups." He paced back and forth beside the table. "You're too wild, too free. You'd feel like a prisoner in their formal houses, bound up in a necktie and underwear. They'd accept you about as soon as they'd accept a Cheyenne." His nose made a wheezy sound. "Or a rattlesnake."

"Mr. Bent!" Charlotte said firmly, stuffing her fists into the folds of calico over her wide hips. "I don't mean no disrespect, Mr. Bent, but Julio here may not be like you a'tall! Not everybody'd choose a dirty old fort in the middle of this godforsaken Injun territory over a beautiful home like your mama's in Missouri!"

"Charlotte! Charlotte," Dick whispered, tugging her sleeve. "Mind what you sayin'!"

"You keep out a this!" She jerked her arm away from Dick. "Mark my words, Mr. Bent. If Mr. Forester is this boy's grandpappy, he'll cherish this chil' til' his dyin' day. Dick and me, we knows how it is to be separated from family."

"Did—did—" Julio felt as if his head would burst. "How long ago were you in Independence? When did Mr. Forester get there? When will ten years be over?"

"Look, Julio." Bent cleared his throat and paced again. "Unless there's some proof, some evidence, forget this! It would be nothing but a wild goose chase. Besides, Myron was already an old man. He may not even be. . . ."

"Hogwash! Nonsense!" Charlotte leaned toward Julio, hands clasped as if in prayer. "Don't you remember nothin' else from before? Don't you have nothin' from that wagon?"

"I may remember a woman with yellow hair, and sometimes I dream a name—Billy—"

"Billy! There!" Her chest puffed up like a mother robin's as she pivoted toward Bent. "An American name!"

"—and I remember a song about love and chickens and bones. And a long time ago Papá gave me a tiny silver coin. Father Martinez said it was an American half dime. I think Papá found it with the wagon. I left it with my sister in Taos. A half dime made in Fil Fil-la Del-fia."

"Philadelphia?"

"Yes! And now I have these things Mamá sent with the sheepherder Helacio." Julio picked up the bundle.

"What's in there, boy?" Charlotte shoved dirty dishes aside, and Julio slid Papá's bundle onto the table. He peeled away Papá's two coarse woolen shirts and Teresita's hand-stitched handkerchief to show the book nestled inside. Gold edging and lettering gleamed in the candlelight.

"Why, honey," Charlotte exclaimed. "This here's a Holy Bible!"

"A family Bible?" Bent rushed back to the table. "In English! This couldn't have been Enrique's! Why didn't you show it to us sooner? Where'd you get this?"

"Mamá sent it with Helacio, and Helacio gave it to me. I'd never seen it before then. I don't know why Mamá and Papá kept it hidden from me." As soon as he'd said the words, Julio realized what he said was not true. "I-I *do* know. Ever since I was little, Mamá said I was her own son, that she was my mother and Papá was my father. I think she was afraid that if I knew, I'd leave." He lowered his head. "And now I have."

"Well!" Charlotte shook his shoulder. "What's done's done! Now open it up!"

The pages had stuck together, probably with dampness from rain and the river crossing. Carefully Julio separated the edges with his ragged thumbnail and peeled the pages apart at the very beginning of the book.

Charlotte moved a candle closer. "Uh-huh!"

Julio pointed to the smeared handwritten ink on the colored lines beneath the scrolls. "What does it say here?"

Bent reached for the Biblc. "Family names, dates of births, marriages, deaths." He flipped back a page, then forward again.

Charlotte's arm lunged over Bent's shoulder. "Yes! See here? Read this, Julio!" Her finger thumped a blurred line. "Here you is!"

Julio stared at the letters, then glanced toward Charlotte.

"Oh! Oh! You poor chile," Charlotte exclaimed. "You cain't read, can you? But you will. If I learned to read, you will too, 'specially with Mr. Forester your grandpappy." Her finger tapped the page. "And he is! It says so right here. This is you!"

"William Allen Forester," Bent read the name aloud. "Well, I'll be! Born May 12, 1830. Mansfield, Pennsylvania."

Julio took the Bible and touched the paper where Bent's finger had found the name. "Am I William Allen Forester?"

"Looks like you are." Bent held the Bible loosely in his hand. "I guess one chance in a million is all you need, Julio. Everyone up and down the Missouri River knows Myron Forester. He's as much a fixture in Independence as the Jackson County Courthouse." He peered down at the names. "I've known him for years. I know all about his lost family, but it never occurred to me that Enrique's son—you!—could be Myron's grandson."

"But, but—" Julio stammered, glancing back to the smeared family names. "But does the book say Billy?"

William Bent chuckled. "Bill, Billy. Nicknames, short for William." Bent clasped Julio's shoulder. "Your real name is William, just like mine."

"Bill. Billy. William." Julio felt as if his moccasins were lifting him off the hard-packed floor. "William Allen Forester." After a lifetime of wondering, he'd finally found out why his eyes were green and his hair the color of straw. "What color is Mr.—my grandfather's—hair?"

"Why, he's an ol' man now, Mr. Julio," Dick said. "It's silver."

"And his eyes?"

No one remembered.

"I was born in 1830?" Julio began counting on his fingers. "1830, 1831, 1832 . . ."

"Fifteen, chil'," Charlotte said. "Makes you fifteen years old."

"Fifteen years old. I came from Pennsylvania, and William is my name," Julio said to himself. In the depths of his soul, a new chant began. Independence. Independence. Independence. "I don't know where it is, or how long it will take me to get there," Julio said, "but I'm going! I'm going to this place called Independence. I'm going to find my grandfather."

4

Julio awoke to the snores and farts and moans of a room full of sleeping men. The workers' quarters were stuffy. He was hot, and his head felt as if it were wrapped in cotton. Julio quietly rolled up his mat and put on his moccasins. Motioning Chivita to come, he slipped outside into the sweet morning air.

The Fort was still quiet, but Julio's mind was not quiet at all. Thoughts and feelings and questions raced at each other, spun and collided—home, war, his Mexican family, his Cheyenne family, his American grandfather in Independence, maybe an unknown family in Pennsylvania. Where did he belong? Could he learn to live in an American house and wear a rope around his neck and eat with a fork? Or was his spirit too wild, too free, the way Bent said?

Julio wondered how his American grandfather would look, how he would talk, how he'd smile. Maybe he'd wear little eyeglasses. "Chivita, we have to find him while he's still there." But doubts tugged, and he added, "Even if we don't stay."

He walked quietly through the entryway to the double gates, slid open the latch, and let himself outside, pulling the gate shut behind him. He followed the Fort wall to the corner, turned, and walked along the south wall with the warmth of the rising sun on his back. Chivita quivered, pointing her nose toward the large herd of Mexican sheep by the river, the sheep Helacio had brought. "No, Chivita, las ovejas are not ours to take care of. At least not yet."

A meadowlark pierced the morning with a warbled song. "That's a good sign." Julio traced a cross over his forehead and chest. Without thinking, he reached to touch the necklace around his neck, then remembered. When he left the Cheyenne, he'd given the bear-claw necklace—and his precious eagle feathers—to Silent Walker to keep until. . . . If I go to Missouri to find my grandfather, will I ever see her again?

Julio found empty wooden molds neatly stacked where they'd been left to dry in the sun. Adobe bricks rested with one edge on top of the next in a zigzag pattern across the ground. A hole, a shovel, dry mud, an overturned wooden bucket, wooden trowels, and nearby a mound of straw covered with burlap weighted down with rocks. Everything he would need was there, as if Papá had left them ready just for him.

Julio slipped off the moccasins Silent Walker had stitched and beaded and rolled up his pant legs. He carried the bucket to and from the river, shoveled the dirt into the hole, then jumped in, mixing river water and dirt into clay. The clay was cool and familiar as it squished up between his toes. He stepped; the clay squished. He stepped; the clay squished. He stepped; the clay squished.

With the rhythm of his feet and the smell of wet clay, his thoughts drifted back to the first time he had made adobe with Papá. He must have been about six or seven; Teresita had just celebrated her sixth Saint's Day.

He remembered losing his balance that morning, falling into the mud. Thrashing around and slipping and sliding, he was covered with sticky clay from feet to shoulders. Mud coated his hands and arms, splashed into his hair, and onto his face—and Papá was laughing—laughing so hard he fell down, too.

You fell on purpose, didn't you, Papá? Julio shook his head. Of course you did. Papá, even if I find my American grandfather, I'll never love you less! Not you or Mamá. I'll never forget. I'll put a marker on your grave. I'll go back to Taos to see Mamá and my sisters.

By the time Charlotte's triangle clanged the morning meal, Julio had finished patching the adobe mix into a crumbling doorway. He blocked off the entrance with a squat wooden bench.

"Well, well! Good morning, Julio. Or should I call you Billy now?" William Bent's voice boomed above him. "The wagons are about to roll."

Julio peered up. This morning William Bent looked different. He was shaved, his hair had been washed and trimmed, and his ironed shirt gleamed in the sunlight. He eyed Julio's patching with an approving nod.

"Mr. Bent," Julio stood, muddy hands hanging. "Are you taking that herd of sheep to Missouri? Chivita and I could drive them for you. We would earn our way."

A flicker of a smile flashed in Bent's eyes. "You? And one sheep dog?"

"At home, we watched the sheep every night."

"Well . . ." Bent ran his fingers across his chin. "I suppose I could recruit a couple of men from the wagons to help out when you really need them. 'Course, they wouldn't like it. Sheepherding's the worst job there is, worse than cooking. I sure would like to get those sheep to my farm at Kansas Landing before winter, though. I'd been planning on it before Helacio went back to Taos." He rubbed his hand over his chin and looked off into the distance. "Ever traveled with a wagon train?"

"No."

"We push hard to get there and back to the Fort before snow falls. Days will be long, nights short. You've got to keep up. And you've got to understand one thing. The trail master is boss. His word is law. You do what he says. Agreed?"

"Agreed!" Julio nodded. "Who is the trail master?"

"I am!" Bent reached out to shake hands, but laughed at the mud and pulled away. "Soon as everything is loaded and the animals are hitched we'll be heading out. Run to the trade room. Tell Red to hurry and fix you up. You'll need everything—hat, boots, everything. Red knows. Cost of supplies will come out of your wages when you deliver those sheep to Kansas Landing."

"Where's Kansas Landing?"

"This side of the river from Independence." Bent was already loping toward the gate, but he turned back and smiled. "Don't worry. You can go on to Independence and see if your grandfather's still there, but the sheep stop at Kansas Landing."

Julio stared down at the adobe hardening on his hands. For a moment, his thoughts, too, seemed to harden like clay. Leaving for Missouri! Today!

"Last spring we were hung up for a month along the way, bogged down in mud, chewed up by mosquitoes. The sheep got footrot, flux. Check the sheep wagon. See if Helacio left everything you'd need in a case like that."

"Sheep wagon?" Julio echoed. "But I need to be walking." He couldn't herd sheep with a wagon! He wished he had a pony.

Bent laughed. "That'd be an awful long walk."

"But I need to be with the sheep. I can't herd sheep and drive a wagon too."

"Let Chivita do the herding," Bent said. "I'll get some men to help if you need it, Julio." Bent tilted his hat back on his forehead and looked up at the sky.

"William!" A man motioned from the courtyard. "They need you out there!"

"Tell them I'm coming," Bent shouted. Then he lowered his voice and walked back toward Julio. "Julio, there's something you ought to know about Myron . . . your grandfather. You know what happened to Don Antonio Chávez?"

Julio nodded. Everyone knew what happened to Don Antonio. Texans had ambushed his caravan out in Kansas Territory and stolen his gold and silver. Then they murdered him and threw his body in a ravine.

"Your grandfather knew that was going to happen. The bandits were local men who had been sitting in Yoacham's Tavern over in Westport all winter drinking and plotting and talking loud. Myron called them banditti, bandits! That's all they were. Bandits. They claimed to be Texas sympathizers, but they were no more Texan than you are. Myron tried to get the dragoons—American soldiers—from Fort Leavenworth to intervene."

"My grandfather tried to stop *that*?"

"Yes, he's that kind of man." Bent's eyebrows raised. "And he would have succeeded too, if the government hadn't been so slow to act."

"But they caught them." Julio said.

"Oh, yes, they caught all but two, took them to trial, and hung the two leaders." Bent shrugged. "But if the United States admits Texas into the Union, they'll be taking on all the problems that the Independent Republic of Texas and those 'Texas sympathizers' have caused. Add that to squabbles over trade policy and idiotic governments on every side. . . ."

"William! Let's get rolling!"

Bent clapped his hand on Julio's shoulder. "Guess what I'm trying to say is this. It's not going to be easy for you in Missouri if war breaks out, but if there's anybody who'd understand how you feel, it'd be Myron. Now, if you're still of a mind to go, get a move on! I'll tell Dick to yoke the oxen."

Julio whacked and scraped his hands together, sending dried chunks of adobe flying. Grabbing the bucket and trowel, he ran from the courtyard to the river, washed them and himself, and put the tools back where his papá had left them. "Papá," he said aloud, "gracias! Thank you, Papá, for giving me my history. My past. War or no war, I'm heading for Missouri."

Both inside and outside the Fort now exploded with activity. Donkeys and mules balked and brayed, oxen waited patiently for wooden yokes. Everywhere trappers and traders called to each other and their animals, rushing back and forth to heavily loaded wagons. Men carried loads of folded buffalo pelts pressed so tightly together they looked like wooden boxes. Julio raced past them into the trade room.

"Red?" Julio panted.

"Well, hello again!" the clerk answered, smiling from behind the counter.

"I'm driving Mr. Bent's sheep to Missouri! He said to tell you, fix me up, and he said to hurry."

Julio could scarcely stand still while Red tossed supplies onto the counter as if there was nothing special about them. Two pairs of American-made pants, two shirts. Soap, a knife, rope, steel and flint, a bandanna. Even matches. Julio had never struck a match before. Candles, fine white beeswax candles. Coffee, hard candy, sugar, flour, leavening . . . more fine new things than he or his family had ever owned piled into one canvas bag, all for him.

"Try them. Put them on." Red shoved the pants and shirts toward him.

Julio scrambled into the American-made pants. They were stiff and rough against his legs, and the shirt rubbed his neck. His feet felt like tree trunks inside the heavy leather boots. How did people live in clothes like this? "And a hat?" Julio asked, eyeing the tall, broad-brimmed Mexican sombrero hanging from a saddle horn in a far corner.

"You want that?" Red laughed, sliding it across the counter. "Somebody lost it or left it here."

"It's like the sombrero Papá used to wear."

Shouts outside the gates grew louder. Red glanced into the courtyard. "Sounds like they're ready to move out," he said, picking up a smoothbore trade rifle and studying Julio quizzically. "Did he say I should give you a gun?"

Julio shook his head.

Red looked down at the rifle and again at Julio. "Do you have a weapon?"

"My slingshot," Julio said, "and my knife. I've never shot a rifle." Still, he thought, a gun would be good protection against dangers on the trail—against Texans or Apaches—or in a war. But Red shrugged and leaned the rifle against the wall behind the counter.

Outside a bell began to ring. Cannon fired from the round bastions on the high corners. Excitement snapped the air with shouts of "Gee!" and "Haw!" and the crack of bullwhips. The wagons were moving.

"Thank you, Red! Adios!" Julio grabbed the canvas bag and darted toward the doorway, stumbling in the heavy boots.

"Wait! You have to sign." Red pushed a ledger and a pencil across the counter.

Julio hesitated.

"Make a mark. Anything will do."

Quickly Julio drew a cross like the one he'd carved on the tree near Papá's grave and grabbed his gear. Outside the door he stopped long enough to work his feet out of the boots, and legs out of the pants, and slipped his tattered cotton pantalones and moccasins back on—much better. He tucked the new clothes into the canvas bag, then ran barechested through the courtyard, and out the gates.

The first wagons were inching ahead while others were maneuvering into position. The sheep would follow. He would check the sheep wagon, then round the herd up—fast—and he would be on his way to his grandfather! "Chivita!" he called. "Vamos, Chivita! Let's go! Ovejas!"

But Chivita was not there. He ran back inside, into the workers' quarters, and grabbed his things. "Chivita, ven!" But she wasn't there either.

Sprinting outside, he tossed his basket and his new canvas bag against the Fort wall and ran along the wagons, calling her name over and over and over again. But there was no familiar yip, no sign.

When had he seen her last? Not while he was patching adobe. Not in the trade room. By the river? Yes! The last time he saw her she was lying under a tree near the hole where he was mixing adobe. But she wasn't there either. She must have gone back inside the Fort . . . somewhere.

"Red!" He darted into the trade room. "Red?"

"Whoa, Julio!" Red exclaimed. "I thought you'd gone! Did Bent send you back for the rifle?"

"No, have you seen my dog?"

Red stroked his beard, shaking his head. "No, I—"

Julio spun around, back into the courtyard, back into the workers' quarters, then to the empty room where the pelts had been stored, then the well room, in and out, first one room, then another. "Dick! Dick Green!" he yelled, skidding into the blacksmith shop. Dick was pulling on the bellows, sending air whooshing into the coals, making them glow white then red. He gripped long tongs holding a metal hinge in the white-hot coals, then placed the hinge on the anvil, lifted a pointed hammer, and with two blows punched a hole. Finally he looked up.

"Dick! Have you seen Chivita?"

Dick rocked back on his heels, tossed the glowing hinge onto the dirt floor, and set the hammer aside. "Well, well, well," he said slowly.

"Dick! The wagon train is leaving without me! I have to find Chivita and catch up. Have you seen her?"

"Well, Mr. Julio," Dick said, without smiling, "maybe you ought to ask mah wife. "Charlotte!" he bellowed, eyes dancing. "Charlotte. He's here." Dick followed along as Julio charged through the open doorway of the smithy.

Charlotte met them in the courtyard, fists punched into the folds of her flowered calico dress. "Well! 'Bout time," she scolded. Then a huge smile uncovered her flashing white teeth. "That lil' ol' dog of yours," she said, "she's under the stairs in my room birthin' puppies!"

"Puppies!" Julio gasped. "Puppies!"

Julio tiptoed into Charlotte's room. "Chivita?" he said softly, crawling under the stairs on his hands and knees.

The dark, safe place underneath the stairs smelled of new birth and damp dog hair. Chivita circled around and around, agitated, craning her neck around to look behind her. Her eyes were opened wide. One tiny puppy squirmed on the floor. It was all one color, a tawny yellow.

Ducking to keep from bumping his head on the bottom of the stairs, Julio scooted closer. "Ahhh, Chivita, your very first puppies. But you scared me. I was afraid I'd lost you." He stroked her head, her ears, and down her neck. "But it's all right now. You're all right. And look what's happening! I didn't see any signs of this." He could feel the muscles rippling inside her belly. "We'll catch up. It'll be all right."

"What you goin' to do, boy?" Charlotte was bending over, peering in. "You best get movin'."

"I'm going, and so are Chivita and her puppies! But I can't move her while she's birthing. And without a sheep dog . . . Ay, I can't herd those sheep and drive a wagon too. No one could! I'll take the wagon and tell Mr. Bent we'll catch up as soon as we can."

"I'll be back, Chivita. Stay. You'll be all right." He scooted out from under the stairs. "Dick, is the wagon ready?"

"It shore is." Dick nodded.

Dick was tugging off his black-leather smithy's apron.

"Now, Dick! What you fixin' to do?"

"You know, Charlotte, it's been awhile. . . . I was jus' thinkin' 'bout goin' for a little wagon ride, make sure them oxen behave."

5

He was breathing hard. Sweat trickled down his temples as he crawled beneath the stairs again. "Mr. Bent says the wagons will wait for us at the Purgatory, Chivita," Julio whispered. "Our gear's loaded, ready to go."

Nose down, almost hidden in her paws, Chivita peeked out from beneath wrinkled brows, then raised her head and laid it back down again. Her eyes were not wild now. She looked calmly at the row of tiny nursing puppies, then back at Julio as if to say, "See? Look what I've done!" Beside the yellow puppy five more lay nursing—one was black, one was a mix of yellow, brown, and white, and three were black and white, just like Chivita.

Julio eased one of the black-and-white pups from Chivita's belly and cupped it in the palm of his hand. "Hello, little one," he whispered, running the tip of his finger over its head. "Where did you come from?" It was so small its face looked squished together, little eyes, nose, and mouth too close to each other to fit. "You're awfully tiny, but you're going for a long, long ride in the back of a wagon."

The pup squeaked.

A tattered blanket landed with a whoosh under the stairs, and Charlotte's voice said, "Carry 'em in this. It'll make a nice, soft bed in that wagon." She laughed. "They's goin' to be one batch of spoiled little puppies, if you ask me! You can count on that!"

"When they grow up . . . uhhh!" Julio's head whacked the bottom of the stairs. ". . . they'll be good sheep dogs, just like their mother."

Julio set the first puppy on the blanket, but when he reached for another, Chivita lowered her head and growled softly. "I'm not going to hurt your puppies, Chivita." Then he said the word she most loved to hear, "Ovejas! We have sheep to herd. Sheep, Chivita! Ovejas!"

Chivita's ears pricked forward.

"What did you say to her?" Dick asked.

"Ovejas. O-*bay*-hus," Julio spoke slowly. "Sheep."

"O-*bay*-hus," Dick repeated, then chuckled as Chivita jumped to her feet and glanced quickly from side to side.

"Vamos," Julio urged. "I'll carry your pups."

Julio gathered the puppies into the blanket, where they rode mewing like kittens in his arms. Chivita trotted along beside him with her head uplifted, never taking her eyes from the blanket.

Dick had pulled the sheep wagon into the passageway behind the blacksmith shop and turned the ox team so they faced the gate. The two oxen had long pointed horns and were yoked together with a large cottonwood yoke. The wagon was a simple rectangular wooden box with a flat canvas cover. Julio tugged the canvas loose in a front corner, hollowed out a place between his new bag of supplies and his basket, and tucked the blanketful of puppies in between. "Bueno, Chivita," he murmured, stooping to pick her up. "Now you can stop whining. See? Your puppies are fine." Gently he nestled her with the puppies and climbed onto the seat beside Dick.

"I'll be back tomorrow, Charlotte," Dick said, as he released the brake. "Soon as Chivita's on her feet." He snapped the bullwhip. "Mah whole life, I work like a dog." He chuckled, flipping the reins. "But this is the first time I ever worked *for* a dog! Herding sheep!"

Julio grinned. "No, Dick. You drive. I'll herd." He rode beside Dick out through the gate.

The sun was already sloping down toward the west. Julio pivoted on the seat to look back at the mountains. "It's like starting life all over again," he said, as he turned to face the prairie that stretched for as far as he could see to the east, toward his grandfather.

"Yessuh, I 'spect it is, Mr. Julio." Dick flipped the reins. "I 'spect it is."

Julio reached into the wagon bed. "It's all right, Chivita." He rubbed her head as the wagon moved toward the flock. "You ride here. Stay with your babies." He pulled out his leather bag and slipped it over his head and shoulder. Everything he would need to care for the sheep was still inside—sling, stones, his flute. He checked the knife at his waist and tested the blade for sharpness.

The sheep began to shuffle nervously as the wagon rolled near. "You'd better stop here, Dick," Julio said. "Once I get them moving, follow us, but not too close."

Julio slipped the new sombrero onto his head, hopped down from the wagon, and walked quietly toward the flock. He stood, relaxed and silent, letting the sheep get used to him. Then, from his leather bag, he pulled out his flute and began to play the calm, soft tones he had played for his flock back home.

From the wagon bed came a whine, then a sharp little bark. He slipped the flute from between his lips. "No,

Chivita," he said, as her head popped above the side of the wagon bed. "Stay!"

He looked over the flock. There must be three or four hundred, he guessed. Some big shaggy ewes still hadn't lambed, others had. Gangly newborn lambs with long tails tottered and raced from their mothers and back again, their hindquarters high, startlingly white in contrast to their grimy elders. How will they ever survive a journey of seven hundred miles? What will happen to them along the way? What will happen to all of us in new territory with Texas spies and hostile tribes?

He didn't know, but for now a hint of dust in the east marked the path of the wagon train, and everything between the dust and the Fort seemed peaceful and calm. And beautiful. Cactus splashed colors of yellow and fuchsia through the greening buffalo grass, and the air was filled with the softness of spring.

Julio turned to the north toward a sand hill that looked like a stack of Mamá's tortillas cut straight through, then glanced back one last time toward Taos and Bent's Fort.

He let the soft heels of his moccasins sink deep into the prairie soil and moved in a slow circle to face the four sacred corners of earth. This time his prayer was more than to Saint Christopher and Santa María, more than to his angel-mother with yellow hair, more than to the spirits of the Cheyenne world. It was a prayer to them all.

He breathed in the sharp fragrance of sage, raised his arms, and sang out, "Bueno, ovejas. *Caminemos.* Let's start walking."

The last rays of sun were spreading a golden-pink hue across the cottonwood trees and willows that lined the river when Julio heard Dick shout. He blinked dust from his eyes and peered ahead. His heart paused, missed a beat, then raced forward. There were Bent's wagons, camped near the river for the night. Wagons—and tipis! Tipis! Could it be?

Could those tipis belong to *his* band of Cheyenne? Was Silent Walker there? Was Néške'e, his Cheyenne grandmother, there? He'd been afraid that he would never see them again.

Sprinting to the wagon and Dick, he said, "Let's circle around and stop downstream where the sheep won't foul the water for the camp." The Cheyenne, Julio knew, would bathe in the river in the morning. He pointed to an area of dense growth under the cottonwoods and willows. On the opposite side, a smaller river joined the Arkansas. "So that's the Purgatory."

"Shore is." Dick nodded.

Involuntarily Julio shuddered. I don't remember this place, he thought, but I've been here before. "The River of Souls Lost in Purgatory. . . ." he said aloud. "I wonder why my parents—my American parents—came here? Where were they—where were *we*—going?" He reached into the wagon bed and let his fingers ripple from Chivita's fur onto the silky coats of the helpless little puppies. "If Papá hadn't found me, I would have died here too."

"Wasn't your time yet, boy." Dick nodded down at him from the driver's seat. His voice rumbled deep in his chest. "You know, the Frenchmen call this river, River of Suffering. It was your time to suffer, but not to die. They was something you was meant to do." A smile spread across his face that was several shades lighter now than when the day began, covered with powdery dust. Even the tips of his eyelashes were light. "Yessuh!" He nodded. "I reckon they's still something important you gonna' do with the days God give you. And I reckon it won't be eatin' dust after a pack a' sheep for long."

Julio drove the reluctant, bleating herd in a wide circle around the camp to the thick undergrowth along the river. The willows and weeds would provide a natural curved corral along one side. He'd build a makeshift enclosure to circle them in.

As soon as he stopped, the sheep quit complaining and nosed into the grass, happy to rest. Julio trotted back to the wagon, looking toward the camp to see any identifying signs on the tipis.

"Stomach's rubbin' mah backbone!" Dick stepped down from the wagon, testing his legs, and stretched his spine. "I'll water these oxen and tie them over there where the grass is long. Then les' go get us somethin' to eat."

"Go ahead, Dick," Julio said. After tonight, with Chivita's help, he wouldn't need to build corrals. But for this first night on the trail, he hoped even a flimsy enclosure would help the sheep feel safe and keep them from wandering. The fence wouldn't have to be strong. "Just something you'll see and think you can't get through," he said, as he pushed his way through the sheep, burrowing his fingers deep into the thick wool, then sniffing the familiar scent that clung to his fingers.

Near the river Julio slipped the knife from his sheath and quickly began to cut and weave willow branches, stabbing the pointed ends into the ground. The semicircle was complete, and it was almost dark when something sharp struck through the thin fabric of his pantalones.

"Ay, Dios!" Julio cried, leaping over the loose pile of branches. Then it struck again, but this time he heard something bounce into the leaves. It wasn't a snake. It was a pebble! Julio's breath caught in his throat. Silent Walker!

His heartbeat, already thumping wildly, beat even faster. Silent Walker hadn't thrown pebbles at him that way for a long time. Before he turned toward her, he made sure his smile was gone.

He squinted toward the river through the near darkness until he saw her figure slip from behind a cottonwood tree. No doubt she was laughing.

She was wearing her fringed brown suede dress that hung longer on one side than the other. Now it was clean. Not a single stain remained. He remembered the terrible scene when he last saw her wearing that dress, just after Dancing Feather was killed in the battle with the Kiowa. She was striking the sharp blade of her knife against her face over and over and over, venting her grief.

"I was afraid I would never see you again," Julio called out. Silent Walker didn't understand his words, at least not many of them. Even if she did, she couldn't answer. Dancing Feather had told him that she wasn't his sister or even his cousin. Néške'e wasn't her mother. She wasn't even Cheyenne; she was Kiowa. The Cheyenne had carried her away after a battle when she was three or four years old, and she hadn't spoken since.

She gestured for him to come.

A summer chorus of locusts began to throb in the cottonwoods, and Julio's blood throbbed with that same

pulsing rhythm inside his ears. The palms of his hands
began to sweat.

Silent Walker stamped her foot. *Come,* she gestured
again.

Julio laughed. Silent Walker hadn't changed too
much. She still threw pebbles. She still stamped her foot.
You come here. He walked toward her, holding out his hand,
trying not to stare at the scabs on her face. Her hair was
still long, glossy blue black as beautiful as a raven's wing.
She still moved with the grace of a doe as she stepped
shyly from the shelter of the cottonwoods. Like a doe, she
stepped, paused, stepped.

"Come, look." Julio led her toward the wagon.
Chivita's head popped up over the sideboards, ears alert,
and she yipped an excited welcome. "Look." Julio lifted
one of the puppies, the yellow one. Its fur was dry now.
Chivita had licked it clean, and its tiny tail stuck up like a
ruffled feather.

Silent Walker's dark eyes widened. She reached for
the puppy, cradled it in her hands, and nuzzled it with her
nose. He reached past her for his bundle and unwrapped
the Bible, now his most precious possession. Carefully he
opened the cover and pointed to his name. "This is me."

Silent Walker frowned and shook her head. She thrust
the yellow pup into his hands, then pointed toward the
tipis. The movements of her fingers were too fast for him
to understand all the signs, but he knew what she wanted.

"No, Silent Walker. I have to stay here with the sheep,"
Julio said, knowing that if he ever spent one more night
with the Tse-tséhésé, the Cheyenne, he might never want
to leave. Not unless Silent Walker went with him. "Silent
Walker," he said, then was at a loss for words. How could

he tell her about his grandfather? "Oh, I wish you could speak! I wish you would try!"

Silent Walker glanced at him, then lowered her eyes.

"Did you understand that?" Julio asked, amazed.

She nodded, eyes still lowered.

"Do you understand me when I speak English?"

Again she nodded, but only slightly.

Julio wished that for one moment he could be inside her mind, to see and hear the world as she saw and heard it. He sneaked a glance her way. Does she really understand? he asked himself. Or is talking with her like talking to Chivita? Chivita understands the deep meaning of everything, but not the words.

The sheep were quiet now. Some were lying down. Lambs were greedily butting hungry mouths against their mothers. Occasionally one would utter a jagged little cry. Night sounds from the camp floated on the evening air— music from a harmonica, laughter. Julio wanted to go with Silent Walker and see Néške?e and Dancing Feather's father, Chief White Buffalo. He wanted to tell Mr. Bent the sheep and wagon were fine, that Chivita would be able to drive sheep tomorrow. But he couldn't leave; he needed to be near the sheep in case of trouble.

He stepped up into the wagon and reached inside the new canvas bag. "*Mo?óhtavè-hohpe*," he said, pulling out the bag of coffee beans that had come with his provisions. *Mo?óhtavè-hohpe* was one of the first Cheyenne words Dancing Feather had taught him. It was the Cheyenne word for coffee, the "black soup" they loved so much. "For you and Néške?e. Tell Néške?e I will see her tomorrow. Tonight I will stay here with the sheep." He signaled as he talked, and by the disappointed expression on Silent

Walker's face, he saw she understood. "Go back," he said, pointing to the camp. But his mouth was saying those words, not his heart. Something had changed since he and Silent Walker first became friends.

6

That night Julio made his bed in the back of the wagon next to Chivita and her puppies. "I'm sorry to do this to you, Chivita." He cut a piece of rope from the coil in the wagon bed and tied it first around her neck, then around his ankle. "But I don't want you chasing after anything tonight. If trouble comes, I'll take care of it." He had tied her to him this way only once before, the night he almost died, just before the Cheyenne found them.

"Good night, Dick." Squirming down onto his sarapes, Julio called through the darkness. "Thanks for helping me today. When you get tired, call me for the next watch."

Julio heard Dick stirring the coals in the campfire; then he heard him sigh. "Man oughta' be out under God's night sky more often, I reckon. Jus' look at 'em stars, sparklin' like coals in a forge. Almost wish Charlotte was here with me."

And I wish Silent Walker had stayed, Julio thought, gazing upward. "Yes," he murmured, "they're beautiful."

Beautiful was the last thing he remembered until his leg jerked and Chivita was growling and tugging at the rope, struggling to jump out of the wagon. "What is it, Chivita?" Julio grabbed the rope and stumbled to his feet. "Stay!" He held tightly to the scruff of her neck.

Before his eyes could focus, he heard the high-pitched cries of a wounded lamb and the pitiful protests of its mother.

His hand dived into his leather bag for his sling and stones. Thuw! Thuw! Thuw! The sling spun beside his ear, and the stones disappeared into the darkness toward the sound with no effect at all. Lambs screamed and bleated; ewes brayed. The thumping of sharp hoofs made the wagon bed tremble.

Dick scrambled onto the wagon seat. "I was watchin', Mr. Julio, but I didn't see a thing! What is it? What's out there?"

Julio held out the limp sling. "It's already gone, I think. Wolves maybe. Coyotes. Fox. It could have been anything. Maybe a bobcat or cougar. They probably picked off a lamb and kept on running. But look!"

Julio's makeshift fence had collapsed. In the starlight, Julio could make out bobbing islands of white moving farther and farther away and hear the plaintive bleating fade. He didn't know how long or how far the sheep would run before they stopped. Some may have run into the river and drowned. Sheep. They don't have better sense, he thought. That's why they need a shepherd.

"I should have stayed awake with you, Dick." He stooped down, cradling Chivita between his knees. She was trembling. "I should have been out there with them."

"Now, Mr. Julio, don't you be frettin'. You cain't go without no sleep! You done what you could, and I done what I could." Dick clapped his hand on Julio's shoulder. "And you'll do the same next time. And the next." Dick lifted the sling from Julio's hand. "Didn't Red give you a rifle?"

Julio shook his head. "I couldn't see anyway. A rifle wouldn't have helped much."

"Reckon not."

"I thought we'd be safer with a wagon train."

"Out here . . ." Dick sighed. "Charlotte, she'll tell you. Out here in this godforsaken land. If it ain't wolves, it's coyotes or cougar or snakes, or Injuns or weather. Wagons don't make no difference 'gainst none of that."

At first light, Julio and Dick studied the damage from the raid—trampled grass, splattered blood and tufts of wool, willow leaves and branches strewn everywhere. Only the two oxen still stood where Dick had left them. Julio untied Chivita and lifted her down from the wagon. Frantically she ran to a trail of bloodstains along the ground, sniffing, searching.

"Well, now what do we do?" Dick scratched through the thick hair on his head.

"You'll help? I thought you were going back to the Fort."

" 'Course I'll help!"

"Then would you take Chivita with you and tell Mr. Bent what happened? Tell him we need some men from the wagons to round up sheep." Julio lifted a salt lick from the wagon bed and tossed it onto the ground. "Chivita knows what to do. You and Chivita and Bent's men go west and north. I'll go east. Herd the strays back here. They like the salt."

Dick nodded. "Mr. Julio, you one good sheepherder!"

"Well, Dick, you will be too." Julio grabbed his sombrero and plopped it onto Dick's head. "And you'd better look like one. Now you *will* be doing a dog's work! Driving sheep, just like Chivita. And she'll be the boss."

Julio peeled the canvas cover farther back on the wagon and found several pieces of lumber stacked along one side of the wagon bed. The wood was meant for repairs, but it was just what he needed. "We'll leave the puppies here." He angled the longest board from the side of the wagon to the ground. "Chivita can come and go any time she wants. Chivita!" he called. "Up!" He lifted her onto the ramp, coaxed her up to the puppies, then lifted her to the ground. "Up!" he said, and she trotted up again without a moment of hesitation.

"Smart dog!" Laughing, Dick shook his head. "B'fore now never thought I wanted a dog, but I shore wouldn't mind havin' one as smart as Chivita."

"Chivita shouldn't work today at all, but it won't take long. Working a little won't hurt her. She'll round up strays faster than any of us, and. . . . Well, Mr. Bent said we'll be pushing hard."

"I'll watch her, Mr. Julio. Don't you worry."

"Bueno." Julio checked the sling in his leather bag. "We'd better get started. Chivita," he called, "ovejas!" Chivita ran down the ramp, eyes eager. Julio made a circle with his hand. "Ovejas, Chivita. Go with Dick."

Chivita leaned forward, ears perked, looking quizzically from Julio to Dick. "Go with Dick. Ovejas! Ovejas!"

"Vamos, Chivita," Dick slapped his legs. "O-*bay*-hus!"

Julio watched only long enough to know that Chivita understood, then turned and followed the river downstream alone.

7

Julio walked quickly along the border of cottonwood trees that edged the Arkansas. His eyes scanned back and forth, following tracks, noticing an occasional tuft of wool. After the scare Silent Walker gave him last night, he watched for rattlers too. Always watch, he reminded himself. Always be careful. No matter how peaceful a day may seem, or how beautiful a night, remember! Wolves, Apaches, Texans. Anything could be lying in wait.

He paused to look back. Ever since Chivita found him again after the Apache attack in the mountains, she had stayed by his side almost constantly. He wanted her to be there too. They were like two halves of one whole. Now, even though they wouldn't be apart for long, he missed her.

But nothing seemed dangerous here. Whatever took the lamb during the night was gone. The day was clear, and the prairie, green from spring rain, was dotted with blooming cactus and white blossoming spires of yucca. Beautiful.

For the first time in days, Julio swung into the long, loping stride that had carried him the many miles from Taos to Bent's Fort. It was his own best rhythm, his alone, not the shuffle-shuffle pace the sheep would set for weeks to come. He passed several clusters of sheep without stopping. First he would find those that had run the farthest, then herd them back, picking up groups of strays on his return.

The warm sun, walking alone, the rhythm of his moccasins thudding against the prairie soil lulled Julio and brought back memories. The sadness covered over by the scurry of activity at Bent's Fort welled up again. His thoughts moved from Dancing Feather to Mamá and his sisters. How would they receive the news of Papá's death? Should he have gone home?

If only I could write! Charlotte said I will learn. Holding a pen like Americans hold forks, his hand would slice across the page, leaving a crooked trail of words for his sister Teresita to track. "I've found what I came to know. It's what we always suspected. I do have an American family. People at Bent's Fort know my father's father, and I'm on my way to Independence to find him. I want to go, but once I'm in Missouri, will he expect me to stay?"

Suddenly Julio realized that he hadn't seen any wandering sheep for at least half a mile. He turned back just as something rustled in the undergrowth beneath the box elder and cottonwoods. Quickly he slipped a stone from the leather bag at his side and cupped it in his sling. Whatever had moved was too large to be grouse or quail. It could be a lamb. He crept forward, his moccasins scarcely making a sound.

Abruptly he froze without knowing why. He had the sense of a strong presence there with him. A breeze brushed across the back of his neck. Dancing Feather? He looked over his shoulder. Is that you? Are you still with me?

As if in reply, Dancing Feather's voice began to chant in his memory. "Nothing lives long, only the earth and the mountains. Nothing lives long, only the earth and the mountains. Nothing lives long." Why? That was the phrase Dancing Feather chanted in the canyon before he was killed in battle.

Warily Julio scanned the waist-high weeds and grasses that thrived in the shade of the trees. Nothing. There was nothing there, no one, but still that feeling held him in place.

Finally he took in a deep breath and shook off the strange foreboding. He couldn't stand like a carved wooden Saint Christopher any longer. Mr. Bent would want to get the wagons moving. Parting the weeds with both hands, Julio crept toward the movement in the grass.

The only warning was a throaty, "Whuff."

Julio froze. "Ay, Dios!" he whispered.

No more than five wagon lengths away a grizzly rose up from the tall grasses, shaggy head wagging. It was feeding on a lamb. Peering at Julio with squinty red eyes, the grizzly lifted itself higher, higher on its hind legs until it loomed above him—two, three, four feet, sunlight glowing on the silver tips of fur.

Julio's blood flamed. Every muscle in his body screamed to run, but he didn't move. He stood his ground, not letting his eyes look directly into the eyes of the grizzly, hoping the lamb had satisfied its hunger. "Santa María," he prayed under his breath. "*Ayúdeme*. Help me."

The grizzly sniffed the air, wrinkling the bloody fur over its nose, showing red, mottled gums and chipped yellowed teeth. Mouth wide open, neck straining forward, it wagged its head and shoulders back and forth, back and forth. It roared, and the stench of its breath hit Julio full force. Dancing Feather! This can't be my time to die!

Julio knew his only chance was a tree. The slingshot wouldn't help at all. Neither would his knife. Slowly, without turning, he reached back with one foot, feeling the ground. Then the other. Another step.

When the grizzly charged, it moved so fast that Julio was stunned. In an instant, the grizzly had covered half the distance between them. Julio spun around, tearing at the undergrowth with his hands, scrambling, running, stumbling. A tree. A tree. The bear was so close he could hear its huffing, feel the rush of heat from its body. The first blow snagged his arm above the right elbow, threatening to knock him off his feet. Julio staggered, ducked, and dodged to his left. Without slowing, he grabbed the tree trunk, abruptly swinging himself around to the opposite direction. The grizzly stumbled on. Then, roaring fury, it turned, swiping out with its huge paws.

Those seconds gave Julio his chance. Hands grabbing, legs pushing, fingernails scratching, he shinnied up the tree trunk. Higher. Higher. The grizzly reared up. Sharp teeth closed around his foot like a beaver trap. Screaming, Julio wrapped his arms around the tree, lifted the other foot, and kicked with all his strength, hitting the bear's nose. Julio's trapped foot jerked free, leaving the moccasin dangling from a broken fang, and he pulled himself higher into the branches, out of reach.

Enraged, the grizzly swiped at the tree. It shook the trunk, then dropped to all four feet and circled, whoofing and swinging its head, and began to sniff through the grass.

Shaking, Julio slowly inspected his arm. Three of the bear's claws had slashed through skin and deep into muscle. He was bleeding hard. Blood gushed from the wound down his arm and dripped from his elbow. Everything outside and everything inside his body trembled from shock and fear. Gradually he felt the pain. His mouth was parched dry; he felt lightheaded. The sound of rushing water swirled in his ears.

As he reached for a higher branch, the grizzly reared up once more. Julio recoiled, clinging tightly to the tree trunk. Then slowly he grabbed a handful of leaves, plastered them against the wound, and held them tightly against his arm to staunch the flow of blood. If I pass out, Julio thought, I'll fall. He'll have me. I'll die. He rotated his ankle to test for broken bones.

The grizzly stared up with its squinty red eyes and huffed.

Julio felt his body growing weaker and dizzier by the moment. The rushing in his ears sounded louder, but he managed to loosen the string around his pantalones. Slowly, carefully he worked the pants down from his waist, over one foot, then the other. He looped the legs around a branch, then around himself, and tied them in a strong knot. If I pass out, he thought, the pants will hold me so I won't fall into the mouth of the bear.

Below the grizzly returned to the lamb, a moccasin dangling from one tooth.

Julio peered through heat waves back in the direction of the camp, fighting to keep his eyes open, hoping that Chivita and Dick and Bent's men would come looking for him . . . soon. The landscape rippled and swayed before his eyes, like a desert mirage. His eyelids drooped. He blinked, nodded, and his head fell forward. I can't—I can't stay conscious—much longer. "Santa María," he prayed. "Papá, Dancing Feather, Teresita, *ayúdenme*. Help me!"

He looked down at his naked body and remembered how the grizzly claw on the leather thong had curled against Dancing Feather's chest. How had Dancing Feather survived that grizzly's attack? Néške?e. Néške?e had treated his wounds. "Without Néške?e's help," Dancing Feather said, "I would have died."

I have to get back to Néške?e!

Julio drew out his knife. The claw wounds throbbed, and his tongue was swelling in his mouth. He gripped the knife handle, and before the stupor washed over him again, he tied his knife to the pull string of the dangling white pantalones so the blade hung rotating in the sun. Flash. Flash. Flash. "Teresita," he mumbled. "Silent Walker . . ." "Grandfather . . ."

Julio forced his eyes to focus on the grizzly below, on the silver-white tips of its fur, and its huge, undulating form that seemed to ripple like water as it moved through the undergrowth. Then the grizzly seemed to separate from itself, and he saw two grizzlies. One rushed toward the tree again, rising up, higher, higher, higher, closer and closer to him. Like a form hidden inside fog, it was changing, changing. The bear, huge now, glowing white, towered twenty feet above the ground, face to face with him. Its teeth were no longer jagged and broken; its massive forearms reached around him.

Julio grimaced, stiffened. His breathing stopped.

With a touch lighter than the brush of a feather, the grizzly's enormous forepaws encircled Julio and drew him close. A jolt, a shiver, and Julio heard Dancing Feather's deep clear voice say one word: "Protector." Then, like inhaled smoke, the white grizzly disappeared.

The last thing Julio saw before his muscles went limp, before the darkness washed over him and pulled him under, was an eagle soaring high in the eastern sky.

8

"You awake now, Mr. Julio?" Julio heard a moan and tried to open his eyes. Something wet poked against his chin. Slowly he realized that he was bouncing along in the back of the wagon beside Chivita's pups, and he was moaning. One of the pups nosed his face again.

"Whoa! Whoa!" The wagon rumbled to a stop. Julio forced his eyes open, squinting into the late afternoon sun. He started to shade his face with his hand, but when his arm moved, pain seared up through his shoulder and down to his elbow. He winced, muffling a cry.

"Néške?e." Julio licked his scaly lips. "Néške?e." He pushed down with his bare foot to boost himself closer to Dick. The claw wounds throbbed and pulled.

He tried to focus on the gashes in his arm, but saw only a blur of white. Vaguely he remembered Dick cleaning and bandaging the wounds. How long ago had that been? He couldn't see if they were oozing pus, or if there were red streaks creeping out from the claw slashes. "Ay, Santa María," he whispered. "Por favor! Please, don't let there be poison in my blood. I don't want to die."

Suddenly he heard the clip clop of large hoofs and saw Bent's hat and the ears of his white mule over the side of the wagon. Bent tugged the brim of his hat lower over his eyes. "How is he doing?" he asked, then answered himself. "Not so good. A grizzly, was it?"

Julio nodded.

"We saw the signs," he grumbled. "Wish we could have gotten it today. We'll track it tomorrow."

Julio's voice came out in a whisper, his throat, dry. "No." He tried again. "No! *Déjelo!* Leave it alone. Let it be! Just take me to Néške'e, por favor."

Julio saw Bent and Dick exchange glances. "She's an old Cheyenne healer," Bent said, shrugging. "Well, you were lucky, Julio. Alone, unarmed, face to face with a grizzly, not many men would live to tell the story."

"*Y las ovejas?*" Julio's words came out in Spanish. English, right now, was too hard.

"Don't worry about the sheep!" Bent shook his head. "We rounded them up. But Julio, you've hexed me! Ever since you came to the Fort, I've had nothing but bad luck! Puppies. A grizzly. Two days, two delays. And now I lose my sheepherder." Bent tugged off his hat and ran the back of his hand over his sweaty brow. "That's a nasty wound you've got. Deep into muscle, almost to the bone. You and Dick take those sheep back to the Fort tomorrow and get Charlotte to doctor that wound."

In his mind, Julio cried, "No!" but he bit the insides of his lips. The only thing that would change Bent's mind would be if Néške'e could treat the wound and break the rising fever. He had to be well enough to travel.

As Bent rode away, Dick Green stepped from the seat and teetered into the wagon bed. "Now, don't you mind Mr. Bent. You ain't hexed nothing! It's not your fault. But he's right 'bout one thing. You one lucky young man, Mr. Julio. If it hadn't been for Chivita and that knife blade flashin', we may never've spotted you danglin' up there in that tree. You could've hung there and bled to death." The wagon creaked as Dick knelt beside him with a bowl. "Now drink this nice and slow. It's all that's left of an old buffalo the scouts killed. Them scouts and some of the Cheyenne braves are still out huntin' for you."

Julio sipped the broth and almost immediately felt his strength begin to return. "I'm not going back to the Fort!" He tried to get up, but his head spun and he reeled against Dick.

"Whoa now! Not so fast." Dick's strong arms eased Julio's shoulders against his knee. "You ain't quite your ol' self yet. You lost a lot of blood."

"Just get me to Néške?e," Julio rasped. "I'll make it. I'll take those sheep to Missouri, and I'll find my grandfather."

Lightheaded, sweating from the fever, Julio curled up beside the sleeping puppies. "I might never have seen you again," he said, touching a tiny black ear. "Where's your mother?"

"With the sheep," Dick answered, as he cracked the whip. "Gee! Haw! Les' get Mr. Julio to this medicine woman of his. I'd worry 'bout that 'cept for what happened to Mr. Bent last winter."

The wagon jerked forward, and Julio lay back, only half listening to Dick.

"Mr. Bent, he nearly died of diphtheria last Christmas, down at the Big Timbers. He was down there camped with his buffalo hunters and the Cheyenne. His throat closed up. He couldn't swallow, couldn't hardly breathe." The wagon wobbled over a swell. "Easy, easy! We got a hurt boy back here. Anyhows," Dick went on, "Bent's wife, Owl

Woman, and an old Cheyenne medicine man—they call him Old Lawyer—saved him. Strung sandburs on strings of sinew, dipped them in marrow fat, and rammed them down his throat with a notched stick. Oooh-eee!" Dick chuckled. "Hurt like tarnation, Mr. Bent said, but when the fat melted off, Old Lawyer pulled those burs out and brought up corrupt matter, dry as tree bark. In a couple of days, Mr. Bent, he was eatin' again. Saved his life."

By the time Dick finished the story, the wagon was pulling into camp and Julio managed to sit up. The wagon train had not moved. Neither had the Cheyenne village. Everyone seemed to be waiting because of him. Even the sheep gathered around the salt lick. As the wagon neared the flock, Julio tensed. His breath hung inside his chest, and his heart drummed a different beat.

Silent Walker was standing where the wagon had been, her hair catching rays of the late afternoon sun. She was wearing her buff-colored leather dress and moccasins like the one he had lost to the grizzly, decorated with red, white, and blue beads. He could see from the moccasin marks in the dirt that she had been waiting there for a long time.

"Whoa." Dick pulled gently on the reins. "You want me to take you to this medicine woman?"

Julio shook his head.

"Then I'll tie these oxen over there by the water."

Julio stood unsteadily, swung his legs over the side and eased himself to the ground. He winced as his arm scraped against the wood and fought back a wave of nausea.

Eyes wide, Silent Walker stepped toward him. When she touched the skin above the bandage with the tips of her fingers, Julio trembled.

Silent Walker made the signs for *bear*—big bear, grizzly— holding her hands beside her ears, then clawing the air. And the sign for *I saw*.

Julio leaned against the wagon. "You—you saw the grizzly too?"

Forcefully she repeated the signs *bear, I saw*. Then she held two fingers beside her eye in the sign for *sleep*.

Julio blinked and shook his head. His arm throbbed; his stomach threatened to turn inside out. It was hard to concentrate. What was she trying to tell him? "Sleep? In your sleep? Did you dream about a grizzly?" Julio repeated the signs, saying the English words even though he knew she probably wouldn't understand.

Silent Walker stamped her foot, and her hands repeated their message fast. *Bear, sleep, I saw*. Her dark eyes flashed as her finger thumped hard against his chest.

"You *saw me?* You *saw* the grizzly attack me?"

She smiled.

"In a dream? Ay, Dios! You mean a vision, don't you?" Julio leaned his head back against the wagon. "Not sleep. *Like* sleep," he whispered.

Silent Walker nodded so vigorously that her braids flipped over her shoulders. She touched Dancing Feather's bear-claw necklace that hung around her neck, then motioned to Julio's arm.

Was she saying she'd seen the grizzly attack in a dream vision? Teresita dreamed like that too, sometimes in her sleep, sometimes during the day even when she was working. She knew things she could not possibly know. But she knew.

With her right index finger, Silent Walker made three slashes across a finger on her left hand, the sign for

Cheyenne, Tse-tsêhésê brave. You, Soaring Eagle. She lifted her hands high into the air, fingers curved like claws, and stood on her tiptoes, hovering over him. *Spirit Grizzly,* she signed.

Spirit Grizzly! Had she seen the white grizzly—the other grizzly—too? Julio's knees threatened to buckle; his eyes drooped closed. Was this all a dream? Was he still hanging in that tree, dreaming? Néške'e . . . I need to get to Néške'e. Where . . .

Something slid between his head and the side of the wagon, tugging his hair. Dancing Feather's bear-claw necklace thumped against his chest, warm from Silent Walker's skin. The word *Protector* echoed in his memory.

"Néške'e," he said, pointing toward the tipis. Getting Néške'e's help was good, he knew that, but he was vaguely aware of warnings that flashed inside his head. No, don't do this! You left the Cheyenne. You can't eat dog. You can't live the Cheyenne way. Go to Independence. Find your grandfather. But when Silent Walker draped his good arm across her shoulder, he leaned against her and slowly they made their way into the camp.

A slight afternoon breeze stirred through buffalo tails that decorated the outside of Néške'e's tipi. Feathers fluttered from the top ends of the lodge poles, and antelope knuckles clinked together in the breeze like hollow bells. Familiar sounds, familiar smells. Julio felt he was returning home—almost.

Néške'e met him, shaking her head. She stood in front of her tipi, short and brown and solid as the earth, looking as if she too already knew what had happened to him on the Purgatory. Her leathery face pulled down into a deep scowl. Her dark eyes showed no trace of her usual humor. "Ohohyaa!" Néške?e scolded.

Néške?e's scolding voice had nagged him back to life once before, back to sight and into a new world. Now she would heal him again.

None too carefully Néške?e ripped Dick Green's bandages off the wounds and jumped back, her heavy body moving as quickly as Silent Walker's. Her hands covered her mouth, and she stared at the marks from the grizzly's claw. Finally she looked away from his arm and squinted into Julio's eyes, peering deeply, intently, her black pupils contracting to tiny black dots.

"Yes," Julio said, his voice raspy. "The wounds are the same as Dancing Feather's." He lifted the bear-claw necklace from his chest, lightly touching the curved claw to one of the ugly deep cuts. "The same."

Abruptly Néške?e grabbed Julio's arm from around Silent Walker's shoulders and shoved him toward the open flaps of her tipi. She followed him inside and motioned him to lie down on her buffalo robe in the center of the floor. As Néške?e barked orders, Julio could hear Silent Walker outside, building up the fire and pouring water. Muttering all the time, Néške?e searched through leather bags and dried gourds, bringing out one shriveled plant, then another, and crumbling them together.

Julio tugged the leather bag from under him, and in spite of the throbbing heat and pain in his arm, he relaxed into the furry robe that held the smell of smoke. Flies buzzed and bumped against the stretched buffalo-leather tipi covering. Locusts hummed in the cottonwoods. His gaze followed a lodge pole up, up, up, to the top of the tipi where it crisscrossed with others and the top flap opened. Then his vision blurred, lost focus. His mind drifted to the first time Néške'e had taken care of him—when he was lost, blind from snow . . . afraid. . . . He was nearly asleep when Néške'e spread the first concoction on his arm and shoulder. He yelped as much from surprise as pain. Néške'e laughed.

Over and over, Néške'e placed one thing then another on the wounds. Then she sprinkled something black that burned like fire—maybe gunpowder. She left it there for so long that the red tinge of sunset had spread across the sky, bringing a warm glow to the tipi by the time she washed it off and spread a smelly concoction of grease and herbs across the wounds.

Night was closing over them when she handed him a gourd of something hot to drink. It was bitter, but Julio choked it down, thanking her. "E-peva'e." He staggered to his knees, then to his feet, feeling the powdery tipi floor under his one bare foot, fending off Néške'e's protests. "I have to find Chivita."

"Chivita," Néške'e repeated, shaking her head. "Chivita, Chivita, Chivita." She pointed to the shadow on the tipi wall, a perfect, shapely silhouette of Silent Walker standing outside. In the only English words Julio had ever heard her speak, Néške'e said, "Woman better!"

Julio flinched and, as quickly as his dizziness would allow, stumbled from the tipi, scarcely glancing Silent Walker's way.

"E-peva'e, Néške'e. Thank you, Silent Walker. Good night," Julio said. He staggered from the Cheyenne camp, passing curious eyes, hearing over and over again whispered names—Soaring Eagle and Dancing Feather and a Cheyenne word he remembered from Dancing Feather, *háhnama*, bear.

9

Julio only reached the grove of trees near Néške'e's tipi before he collapsed the first time. What herbs had Néške'e put in that tea? He fought the overpowering urge to sleep. He had to watch the sheep. Chivita, where was she? Chivita!

He staggered to his feet, mumbling, "I can't sleep. Not yet! Have to . . . have to make us safe for tonight . . . for tonight. . . . Drive away the grizzly. No grizzly . . ." Leaning on one tree trunk after another, he stumbled on to the edge of the cottonwood grove and out into the clearing. The sheep were calm, sleeping as if the grizzly had never been there at all.

He reached into the leather bag at his side for his flute, but felt Teresita's smooth white stone. Teresita, Teresita, I'm still alive, Teresita. Your magic stone has kept me alive. Do you still have my coin? Pray for me, Teresita. I don't want to die. His fingers touched the sling, the rocks, and finally pulled out the reed flute. Like a part of himself, the flute fit into his fingers, its lip against his. Even though blowing through it made him even more lightheaded, he stumbled on, playing, walking—moccasin foot, bare foot, moccasin foot, bare foot—circling the flock. The ritual was the same one he and Chivita had followed for years, enclosing the sheep in a tight circle, calming them, protecting them from the fears of the night with the flute's quiet song. He glanced about, searching again for Chivita, then remembered groggily, No, she's not here. She's in the wagon. With her puppies. Tonight I will protect the sheep! "Ay, Dios!" he prayed, and briefly his mind cleared. "The grizzly knows where to find easy kill. Please keep him away! Keep the sheep safe. Keep us all safe."

His knees gave way. He sank down, still holding the flute, still continuing to play, letting the flute speak. His song traveled across the mountain peaks to Teresita and Mamá and his baby sister, Gabriela Ultima, and all his other sisters back home. It whistled through the grasses in the field where he heard the bell from the Taos church ring. It paused at the wounded aspen that marked Papá's grave. It was a song of softness and awe, of wonder and gentle discovery, of his journey to Bent's Fort, of the mysterious canyons, of eagles and friendship and death. Tears wet his face as the flute cried once again for Dancing Feather and at the thought of leaving Silent Walker. In his stupor, he fought away sleep with the growling sound of the grizzly, the soaring sound of the grizzly spirit. As he played, his mind danced with the music of his spirit and the longing in his soul. Someday. Someday soon, Grandfather. Someday, Teresita. Someday, Silent Walker soon . . . soo-o-o-n . . . soo-o-o-o-o-nn. . . .

The flute song faded into night. All the sounds, all the memories, all the dreams funneled into a place deep inside, far away from pain. His last conscious connection to the outside world was a shadow . . . a shape . . . a vision . . . someone kneeling beside him.

"Get back!" In the darkest part of the night, Julio awakened shouting, heart pounding, fists clenched. He sat bolt upright; pain throbbed in his arm. Only slowly did he realize that the grizzly was not chewing. He was in a dream, only in a dream.

He lay back again, but his blood was rushing, his nerves standing at attention. Locusts thrummed like the pulse of a heartbeat—one, two, three, four, five, six times, sometimes more, then became suddenly quiet only to start up again. The wings of a nighthawk ripped the air, an owl hooted, fish slapped the surface of the river.

His eyelids became heavier and heavier, and as he sank once again under the effects of Néške'e's tea, his mind wandered back to the grizzly, the second grizzly. The white grizzly. Why did it say, "Protector"? Why would a spirit protect him . . . from what? For what? Was it Dancing Feather? The white grizzly, it must have been a phantom . . . but so real . . . so real. . . .

"Ugh!" Julio awoke with a start, blinking into the early rays of the morning sun. Néške'e kicked his leg again. She was grinning, stretching wrinkles and scars, flashing her brilliant white teeth. A jumble of Cheyenne words tumbled from her mouth. Her dark eyes sparkled like sunlight on the ripples in the river.

Julio sat up and rubbed his hand over his face. He was lying on the ground by the sheep, and his fever had broken. A mourning dove cooed in a nearby tree above him; a magpie squawked. What was happening? Why was Néške'e so excited? "I'm better, Néške'e! E-peva'e."

Tse-tsèhésè. Néške'e traced the first finger of her right hand three times across the first finger of her left hand, then made the sign for *family*. She jabbed his good arm, then her own chest, and pointing toward the tipis shook a handful of eagle feathers. *Feathers horse trade,* she signed.

Julio had no idea what she was trying to tell him. He eased up, brushing sheep droppings and bits of leaves and dirt from his clothes, and picked up the flute that had fallen beside him.

Néške'e nodded to the flute and again smiled more broadly than he'd ever seen her smile before. Her feet danced in the fallen leaves. Again a stream of Cheyenne words rushed past his ears, but he understood only that they had something to do with the flute.

Julio turned toward a rustle in the undergrowth beneath the cottonwoods. Radiant in the slanting sunlight, Silent Walker glided toward him. She was carrying the coffeepot he had given her in thanks for the moccasins, the moccasin his grizzly had claimed. She was more beautiful than ever, dressed as he'd never seen her before, in a dazzling white-leather dress and white-laced leggings. The strands of her hair gleamed with hues of brown and black and deep indigo. The look in her eyes was different too, warmer, less shy, less afraid. He hardly noticed the scabs. But the battered, dented coffeepot jarred memories—his first sight of it, shiny and new, in the donkey's pack in the Plaza of Taos, the campfire with Papá, the Apache raid. It was all he'd had to dig Papá's grave. It was all he had to give as his first awkward gift to a girl— a woman.

The aroma of the coffee reached him ahead of Silent Walker. She knelt, poured coffee into a dried gourd, and handed it to him, her eyes sparkling. Then she gave him dried meat. When he finished eating, she took the feathers

from Néške'e, and the two women led him back toward
the Cheyenne camp and more smiling faces. On the ground
lay a beautiful buffalo robe—a silk robe—the most valued
of all buffalo hides because of its texture and color. "For
Soaring Eagle and Silent Walker," Néške'e gestured,
beaming.

Silent Walker extended both hands toward Julio,
holding the eagle feathers. They were the feathers he had
given her, he was certain, the eagle feathers he and
Dancing Feather had plucked from live eagles in the
canyons to the south. Those feathers were valuable; a
handful could be traded for a horse. Feathers for horses.

The realization crept in slowly. Néške'e and Silent
Walker had brought him breakfast, but he felt as if a huge
boulder had sunk to the pit of his stomach. His mouth
suddenly became dry. Others of the Cheyenne village were
gathering around, all in high spirits.

Néške'e jabbered something at him, impatiently
gesturing for him to take the feathers from Silent Walker.
Then, even more impatiently, speaking Cheyenne and
signing, she made him understand. He was to take the
feathers. He was to trade them for horses. He was to give
the horses to White Buffalo.

Briefly Julio's thoughts escaped eastward. My
grandfather is wise like White Buffalo. What would he do
now? But the voice of White Buffalo himself pulled Julio
back to the moment at hand.

"It is good, Julio!" White Buffalo moved through the
crowd toward him speaking English. "You have returned."
He smiled, not now the caller of spirits in a sweat lodge,
not now the counselor, the chief, the bearer of bad news.
He spoke this time, Julio realized, as the father, adoptive-

father, of Silent Walker. "You play the flute well, Julio," he said. "The village heard your song." His eyes crinkled at the corners as he glanced at Silent Walker with a brief look of tenderness. "All the village knows she went to you. She will make a good wife, Julio. You will make a good husband."

Stunned, Julio stared at the outstretched feathers on Silent Walker's palms as White Buffalo translated his words from English to Cheyenne for his people. Julio looked up into Silent Walker's now-fearful eyes. The feathers resting on her palms quivered.

Ay, Dios! What have I done?

He didn't know exactly, but Julio realized that if he didn't take the feathers—and take them soon—Silent Walker would be disgraced, dishonored, humiliated.

And if he did, he would be married.

10

Julio didn't take the feathers. Neither did he turn away from Silent Walker's fearful gaze. Instead, he placed both of his hands palms down on top of hers, trapping the feathers in between. "Silent Walker," he murmured, leaning toward her, "come with me." He moved to her side, still resting one hand on top of hers, still touching the feathers.

He led her deep into the cottonwood grove by the river where no sheep or horses had grazed, away from wondering eyes. Leaning forward, he spoke to Silent Walker in a half whisper, glancing nervously from the village to the bustle of activity around the wagons. Men were rushing, shouting, hitching up oxen and mules. They would be pulling out soon.

"Silent Walker," he said, "I don't want to shame you in front of White Buffalo and Néške?e or any of our Cheyenne family."

Warily Silent Walker stepped away.

Julio swallowed hard. "I can't take the feathers, Silent Walker. I can't offer White Buffalo horses for you. Not now. First there is something I must do. I have to go, and I don't know if I will ever return." He lifted his hand from the feathers on her palm.

Silent Walker's head lowered, hiding her face. When she looked up, a tear fell from the tip of her nose. Holding the feathers like a flute, she lifted them and blew. Her expression asked, "Why?"

"I'm sorry." Julio touched the rounded point of her chin. "I didn't know playing my flute meant anything! I always play the flute to calm my sheep. I didn't know it meant something special to your people!"

Silent Walker lowered her head once again and turned her face away.

"I have to go to Independence!" Julio made the sign for *father's father*. "I showed you the book with my name. It's from my people. I don't know if they will accept me, but I have to find out who I am when they call me Billy."

Silent Walker's long lashes pressed against her scarred cheeks. Her lips clamped together.

"You must understand! Silent Walker, you're not Cheyenne any more than I am! Dancing Feather told me. You were born Kiowa. The Cheyenne took you just the way Papá took me. You weren't raised by your own family either."

The index finger of Silent Walker's right hand shot out, striking her left index finger once, twice, three times.

"*Tse-tséhése?*" Julio's voice rose. "I know you're Cheyenne now! But before?"

Silent Walker slashed the air with the sign *NO* and ran, her feet swishing through the tall grass.

Julio called after her. "Silent Walker, don't you want to know?"

Silent Walker slowed to a walk, stopped and turned, but not to face him. She pointed toward the east. Then

Julio heard the vibration of pounding hoofs and the excited cries.

"Pawnee! Pawnee!" A Cheyenne brave and one of Bent's scouts galloped between him and Silent Walker and into the middle of the camp. "Trapped in the Arkansas!"

Cradling his arm against his chest to ease the pain, Julio walked as gently as he could into the camp. Silent Walker followed a few paces behind. From every direction, people rushed from tipis and wagons to hear the jumble of shouted Cheyenne and English. Braves grabbed rifles, bows and arrows, spears and shields, leaped on their small ponies, and galloped toward the white smoke that billowed up from a point on the horizon. Several of Bent's scouts and hunters jumped astride their big horses and raced away with them.

Bent leaped up onto the seat of a wagon. "Well, folks," he shouted, "the scouts didn't find Julio, but they did find Pawnee. Spotted the Cheyenne's old enemy on an island digging white clay. White Buffalo's braves sneaked up and started a grass fire." Bent laughed. "It's nothing for you to worry about, but anyone who wants to can ride ahead with me and watch the fun."

Fun! Why would Mr. Bent say that? That kind of fun was what cost Dancing Feather his life.

"Rest of you," Bent yelled, "follow along in the wagons."

The women, children, and old men in the Cheyenne camp were already rushing to leave. Tipis were becoming travois. Lodge poles dragged the ground behind horses, and buffalo hides that had covered the tipis now stretched between the lodge poles to carry belongings. Muleteers and ox drivers tugged animals and harnesses together, and everywhere small campfires were being doused and stomped out. I thought I was saying good-bye, Julio thought, glancing at Silent Walker, but now the Cheyenne village will travel downstream too. The tightness in his chest released.

"Why, Mr. Julio!" Dick Green stepped up beside Julio, looking from Julio's wounded arm to Silent Walker and back again. "I didn't 'spect to see you up and about this mornin'. For someone who tangled with a grizzly, you not lookin' too bad. Pale, but not too bad."

Julio would not tell Dick that each time he moved, his arm felt as if lightning seared through the muscles. He wouldn't tell him that it was hard to move his fingers or anything about the nightmares. "Néške²e and Silent Walker treated the wounds." He turned toward Silent Walker, but that quickly, that silently, she had slipped away. He glimpsed a flash of white leather disappear among the collapsing tipis.

"I have to get back to the sheep before they spook." Julio limped back toward the flock, stepping carefully on his bare foot. A cactus spine would only add to his misery. Before Dick leaves for the Fort, he thought, I'll ask him to pull the American boots on for me.

"When are you going back, Dick? You can't go alone, not with the Pawnee and Cheyenne fighting like this. Anything could happen."

"Uh-huh." Dick nodded his head. "And I s'pose that tells me what you're fixin' to do. You ain't goin' back to the Fort, are you?"

"I'm taking the sheep to Missouri."

"You know"—Dick's voice rumbled deep in his chest—"I reckon I'll just go on to Missouri with you. Kinda' have a hankerin' to see civilization again anyhows, and maybe you could use a hand with them sheep."

"Dick!" Julio shouted. "Do you mean it?"

"Yessuh." Dick chuckled.

"I need another hand, or two, or three! I don't know how Chivita and I could take care of all those sheep by ourselves now." Julio glanced down at the wound. "But what about Charlotte? You told her you'd be back."

"Now don't you be frettin' none about Charlotte. She'll know." Dick smiled. "What about Mr. Bent?"

"Well—" Julio remembered what Bent had said about being boss. He glanced at the second group of riders stirring up dust to the east. "He's not here to ask, is he?"

Dick's head lowered, but Julio could see he was hiding a laugh.

Julio had just stored Chivita's ramp in the wagon bed with the supply of willow staffs he had quickly cut and bent. Dick was cracking the bullwhip to start the oxen when a movement among the trees caught Julio's eye. It was Silent Walker, running fast. She was no longer wearing white leather.

She slowed as she neared the sheep and walked the rest of the way to Julio. *I walk* she signed, shaking her braids over her shoulders. *Here.* Frowning at Julio's boots, she moved around him to the side with the uninjured arm.

How could she be so . . . so good? He'd embarrassed her in front of the whole village. He'd yelled at her, trying to make her understand why he had to leave. He wished she'd never heard his flute, but now? What might happen if he came back at the end of summer? He glanced at her from the corner of his eye and smiled. She was shooing stragglers with widespread arms.

Julio was thankful now for the slow pace of the sheep. Each step he took sent a throb of pain through his arm and shoulder and up his neck into his jaw. It was worse now wearing boots. At least, he wouldn't have to walk back and forth behind the sheep all day. Chivita could tend the flanks while he brought up the rear. And, he admitted to himself, Silent Walker was a good helper.

"Silent Walker, watch!" Julio pointed to one of the bossy ewes eyeing the grass that she was being forced to leave. He could see she was about to bolt. "Watch Chivita."

Chivita had already spotted the problem. In a dusty blur of black and white, she raced toward the ewe and squared off. Head lowered, jaw extended, Chivita fixed her eyes on the ewe, stopping her cold. The ewe feinted to the right, but Chivita anticipated that attempt at escape, and the next, and the next, never breaking the eyehold. Suddenly the old sheep turned tail and scampered back to the flock.

As the wagons and sheep approached the island, heavy smoke from burning grass enveloped them. The smell was strong and needle sharp against the inside of Julio's throat, making him cough, and each time he coughed his arm contracted in pain. His eyes stung and watered.

Rifles popped from inside the smoke. In the distance, Cheyenne warriors bent low over their ponies. They galloped ghostlike back and forth along the bank of the river, appearing and disappearing in a haze of white, yelling and taunting the trapped Pawnee.

By the time the wagon train emerged from the cloud of smoke, the skirmish was over. The strength Julio had felt in the early morning was quickly draining away. The heavy boots were rubbing his feet raw. He stumbled. Silent Walker ran to his side and again draped his good arm over her shoulder. Her eyes were bloodshot and red from the smoke.

"Is this just a game to them, Silent Walker? A sport I'll never understand? Don't they know this is how Dancing Feather died?"

Silent Walker drew a sharp breath and looked away.

Several Cheyenne braves raced past. Bent plodded by on his white mule beside a Cheyenne who was holding his jaw. "What happened?" Julio called out.

"A bullet caught Chief Whirlwind," Bent called back, "right in the jaw. Knocked out a handful of teeth." He turned in the saddle. "Keep a sharp eye out. A Pawnee was killed."

Julio groaned. Another senseless death! And it meant that now, more than ever, the Pawnee would be intent on revenge. He shook his head. He was lightheaded, dizzy. With each step, he wondered if his foot would move forward one more time. At least, Bent seemed to have forgotten— or was ignoring—his orders for Julio to take the sheep back to the Fort. Finally Silent Walker stepped squarely in front of him, stopped, and pointed to a stump. He sat, and Silent Walker signaled Dick to stop the ox team.

Chivita came running to Julio's side, sniffed his hand, then looked away from him to the sheep, eyes moving back and forth between the sheep and the wagon, whining. Silent Walker scooped her up and set her with her puppies in the wagon bed. Then she narrowed her eyes at Julio and pointed to his ponchos spread on the floorboards.

"No, I can't—" Julio started to protest.

But Silent Walker was as intent as Chivita with the sheep. She stomped her foot and jabbed her finger once more toward his bed. Then she pointed to herself and the sheep.

"She's right, Mr. Julio." Dick twisted around on the wagon seat. " 'Member what's happened to you. You're tuckered out. You got to rest. Regain your strength."

Julio didn't remember the wagon starting to roll again. When he awoke, it was night and starlight cast a white sheen on Chivita and her sleeping puppies beside him. He sat up and saw a new campground near the sheep. The campground covered a smaller area than the last, tipis and wagons closer together. The dying embers of small cooking fires glowed here and there like red eyes on the ground, and only the usual night sounds carried through the air—the occasional thump of a horse's hoof, a nicker, a lamb bleating. There was no music, no beating of drums. He wondered why the Cheyenne weren't celebrating their victory. What had awakened him?

The musical seesaw of crickets suddenly became silent. Water splashed nearby. Chivita's head shot up, and she growled softly.

A Pawnee brave, dripping wet, emerged from the willows along the river, crouching low. The silvery light from the stars gleamed on his long-bladed knife.

Julio gripped Chivita's head. "No!" he whispered. "Stay." She would be no match against an armed Pawnee.

The brave scanned the sheep, but he was looking for horses to steal, Julio realized, not sheep. He sprinted closer. Startled sheep bleated. Chivita yipped, and the brave spotted Julio.

Julio reached for his sling, forgetting the bandage that held his arm tight. With only one good arm, he couldn't hold Chivita and handle his knife. He sat, clutching Chivita, suddenly sweating.

The brave stood motionless, wild-eyed, knife raised. In the strange silvery starlight, Julio's eyes locked with his. Julio could hear the Pawnee's breath wheezing in and out and smell the smoke in his wet hair. A dark track of blood oozed from the zigzag wound on his forehead.

Suddenly the brave dashed forward. Fast as a striking rattler, his hand shot over the wagon bed and slapped Julio's bare chest. Chivita lunged at his arm, but the brave pivoted and disappeared back into the willows.

Julio's heart pounded. The brave had counted coup. By touching the enemy, he had earned a great honor, greater than having stolen a horse, even greater than if he had taken Julio's life. Everything happened so fast that it hardly seemed real, but the brave was real, as young and as alive as Dancing Feather had been. And no harm had been done. No one had been hurt.

"Let's keep it that way." Julio eased himself back down onto his bed. "If we tell anyone, they'll go after him," he whispered, pushing Chivita gently onto her side by the whimpering pups. "This will be our secret."

11

At first light, Julio was awake. "Gracias a Dios," he murmured, "for a good sleep." He stretched. His arm was stiff, but the burning soreness had lessened. Nothing more had happened during the night. No Pawnee, no grizzly, no nightmare. Only a good dream that brought a clear message about what he should do the very first thing this morning. Today Bent's wagon train would move on without delay. But the Cheyenne?

"Watch the sheep while I say good-bye, Chivita, and get ready for a surprise."

Chivita cocked her head as if she were trying to understand.

"Never mind." Julio laughed, and scratched behind her ear.

He crawled down from the wagon and tiptoed quietly past Dick, who lay sleeping under a cottonwood tree, one arm covering his face. Had he been there when the Pawnee brave crept into camp? If he had, it was a good thing he slept soundly.

Near the riverbank, Julio kicked a yucca plant onto its side and stepped on the spiked leaves with his heavy boot. He used his knife to cut yucca root from beneath the ground, then knelt beside a shallow eddy in the river. One-handed, he soaped and scrubbed with the root where he could reach. It would have been easier to jump into the water, but he was still wearing the boots that he couldn't pull off one-handed.

Back at the wagon, he searched through the new bag of provisions for a comb and two wax candles. He combed his hair, then combed it again, and slid the candles into the leather bag with his flute and sling.

How can I feel so much sadness and so much excitement, both at the same time? Carrying his secret of the Pawnee brave, he headed toward the camp to find Néške'e and Silent Walker.

His pulse raced when he saw Silent Walker sitting in front of the tipi. She was wearing her buff-colored leather and a smile, but her eyes looked strained and tired. She held out a pair of finished moccasins with a beaded geometric design not like the red, white, and blue lines on his first pair. This design was part bear, part eagle. The head, in profile, had a curved yellow beak and a red bead for the eye. A lump rose in Julio's throat. How could she have done all that in such a short time? She must have worked all night.

Silent Walker tugged off Julio's heavy boots, then jumped away, holding her nose and pointing. No wonder his feet hurt. There were blisters on his heels and red raw spots on his toes. Gently she slipped on the new moccasins.

Julio's voice caught in his throat. He wiggled his toes and knelt to touch the soft leather, running his fingers over the beads. They felt like warm butter on his feet, just like his first pair. "E-peva'e, thank you. And thanks to you—and Néške'e—for working on the silk buffalo robe. Maybe someday—" He stopped himself just in time.

Julio could tell Silent Walker didn't understand his last words. He didn't expect her to. The Cheyenne had done so much for him, and yet he was turning his back on them—on her. The feelings he had for Silent Walker were new and strange and confusing. She wasn't just a friend, and he wasn't just a boy any longer. He wished Teresita were here to help him understand. How could he not come back to Silent Walker? It would be like not coming back for Chivita, but so much could happen between Bent's Fort and Missouri. He couldn't promise Silent Walker anything. A promise would be even more unfair than leaving things the way they were.

Silent Walker smiled. She stood and looked around the village. No one was preparing to leave, but shouts and clanging warned Julio that the wagons would be rolling soon. She pointed to a tawny-colored dog lying in the shade of White Buffalo's tipi. "Ba-bá," she said very slowly, very carefully, a little louder than a whisper as she pretended to hold a puppy.

"Babá?" Julio frowned. "Oh, you mean, papá! The puppies' papá! Ay, Dios!" Blood rushed to his face as he suddenly realized what had happened. "You spoke, Silent Walker!" He grabbed her hands and squeezed them against his chest. "You can do it! You can talk!"

He glanced at the brilliant morning sun, already well above the horizon. William Bent was hurrying drivers to the wagons. "Oh, Silent Walker! You did it! While I'm gone, learn! Learn English. Learn Spanish and French. Listen to everyone the way my sister and I did in the plaza of Taos. Learn every language you hear." He dropped Silent Walker's hands and backed away, breaking into a run. "I wish I didn't have to leave right now. But I do. I have to talk with White Buffalo before I go."

"White Buffalo, I'm sorry about Silent Walker—the flute—I didn't know—" Julio tried to swallow, but his mouth was dry. "I have to go to Missouri. I have to find my grandfather, then—"

"You are a fine young warrior. Follow your path," White Buffalo said. "One day you will return to the land of the grizzly."

Julio looked into eyes that gazed back into his but seemed to see beyond. "Dancing Feather has been with me since . . . since he died. . . ."

White Buffalo nodded.

". . . with the grizzly . . . and other times. Last night I dreamed of his pony. May I take Dancing Feather's pony, White Buffalo? I think he wants me to have it. A pony to help Chivita herd the sheep?"

White Buffalo listened carefully, but without any expression on his face. "When a Cheyenne warrior dies, his pony goes with him to the next world, the Cheyenne way."

Julio heard the words, but he had to repeat them to himself before he could comprehend. "His pony, Dancing Feather's pony, was sacrificed?" His stomach tightened. The Cheyenne way, the Cheyenne way. Will I ever understand the Cheyenne way?

"They are together," White Buffalo said. "Come."

White Buffalo led Julio to a herd of grazing ponies. One speckled pinto mare looked up. Her ears pointed forward, and when her eyes met Julio's, her nostrils flared. She shook her head and trotted up to him as if they were old friends. "This pony chooses Soaring Eagle," White Buffalo said, nodding, using Julio's Cheyenne name.

"E-peva'e, White Buffalo, thank you." Julio ran his hand down the mare's neck, over her prickly-smooth hair. "Pinta," he said, as the mare pushed her head against his shoulder. "I will call you Pinta." He rubbed her soft muzzle.

White Buffalo gave Julio a braided buffalo-hair bridle, and as Julio slipped it over Pinta's flicking ears, something stung the back of his leg.

"Silent Walker." She was throwing stones again. He turned. Néške'e was with her, and Silent Walker was clutching his old moccasin against her dress. Behind them wagons were rolling, drivers shouting, "Gee!" and "Haw!" and cracking whips.

Now that he'd reached the moment of final good-bye, he couldn't say anything more to Silent Walker or Néške'e or White Buffalo. His throat tightened; there was a salty tingling deep behind his eyes. He handed each woman a white beeswax candle, raised his hand to White Buffalo, and led Pinta away.

12

At first, Pinta pranced and tugged at the rope as Julio led her toward the milling sheep. He wouldn't try riding until he was out of Silent Walker's sight. Her last memory of him would *not* be falling off a pony.

In the Cheyenne camp, another pony whinnied. Pinta answered, tugging her head far to the side, trying to shake off the rope.

"I know." Julio stroked her neck. "I know." Julio fought the impulse to turn back too. The village would not be here when he returned. The Cheyenne came and they went; it was their way. Would this be the last time he would see the people who had saved him and Chivita, the last time he would see Silent Walker? Ever?

He was still looking over his shoulder at Silent Walker and Néške'e when Dick pulled the wagon alongside Pinta. "Charlotte told me you lived with them."

Julio answered, "They saved my life."

Dick didn't say anything for a while. He rode, relaxed on the wagon seat, holding the oxen's reins loosely in his hands. Then, as if he were reading Julio's mind, he said, "It's hard, not havin' a place where you know you belong."

Julio nodded, grateful for Dick's quiet understanding.

"Pretty little pony," Dick said, smiling.

"Her name's Pinta." Stroking Pinta's neck, Julio scanned the slowly moving sheep for Chivita. "Pinta and Chivita will have to get used to each other."

"And what about Pinta and Mr. Julio?"

"We'll have to get used to each other too." Dick must have guessed that he didn't know how to ride. When the two figures near the tipi blended into the hues of brown and tan weeds and soil and trees, Julio led Pinta toward the river, found a log to step on, and slid his leg over her back. Her skin rippled and quivered as if she were shaking off a fly. She stomped one foot, then blew through her nostrils. "Easy, Pinta," he said, gripping with his knees. He sat for a while without moving, waiting to see what she would do, then nudged her gently with the heels of his moccasins, released the tension on the reins, and breathed a sigh when she didn't run. "Good, Pinta. Good." Gradually his spine relaxed, and his muscles softened.

The first few times Pinta danced, Julio was startled. For no apparent reason, she broke rhythm and pranced sideways with mincing little steps. There was no rattler, no prairie dog or badger hole. Chivita learned quickly to stay away from Pinta's hoofs. By the time they reached their next stop, Big Timbers, Julio had learned to relax with her dances, proud that she hadn't bucked him off or brushed him off, or he hadn't just fallen off. Not bad for a one-armed beginner, he thought. He was less skittish too of every dark shadow that could be a grizzly. Could Pinta outrun a grizzly? He didn't know, but she would certainly catch the scent and shy away before she came too close.

"Dick!" Julio trotted back to the wagon. "The sheep will like this place!" He turned and rode beside Dick through a meadow of bright yellow sunflowers into the cool canopy of Big Timbers. Behind them, the sun was setting in a crimson swash, casting a pink hue across the tree trunks and under the leaves. The grass was green and dotted with blossoms. The cottonwood trees were larger than any he had ever seen. Holding hands, all his sisters couldn't reach around some of these giant cottonwoods. Big Timbers was a perfect name.

Cook fires were already burning, and as Julio passed by his fellow travelers, it seemed that everyone had heard his story. "How is your arm?" "How did you ever escape from a grizzly?" "How are the puppies?" "Are you really Myron Forester's long-lost grandson?" That evening after dinner five visitors came to the sheep wagon to see Chivita's puppies. Chivita guarded her brood proudly at the same time that her ears and nose tugged her toward the baas and bleats of the sheep.

By the end of the next day, trailing the wagons, Julio could tell that Pinta was the perfect pony for a sheepherder, the perfect pony for him. She already seemed to know how to outwit and outmaneuver sheep. A slight touch of the knee, a word, and Pinta responded. Sometimes she knew what to do even before Julio did and took the lead. Julio suspected that with Chivita's darting and nipping and staring at the sheep, Pinta was learning from her too.

Two days after they left Big Timbers the monotony of the trip set in. From sunrise to sunset, day in, day out, the sheep were on the move. Wistfully Julio thought of the green field near Taos where the sheep browsed and slept and gave birth to lambs without the pressure of constantly moving.

The Rocky Mountains sank lower and lower on the western horizon until they disappeared from sight entirely. Now plains stretched around them so far and so flat that the sky seemed to reach down and tuck under the edges. As he rode, time and time again, Julio's thoughts drifted to Silent Walker. What might have been if he had stayed? What might be if he returned? His mind jumped ahead. He wondered about Independence and Grandfather. And war. Then his thoughts jumped back again, all the way home to Taos. By now, Mamá and his sisters could have heard what happened to Papá.

Along the trail from Big Timbers to Chouteau's Island, one ewe or ram, then another, rebelled and peeled away from the flock, taking others along. Pinta and Julio worked one side; Chivita worked the other. Behind them, stoop-shouldered, Dick drove the sheep wagon, still wearing Julio's Mexican sombrero.

Chivita herded sheep until her tongue lolled. During the break at midday, she collapsed, panting, in the shade of the wagon to nurse her puppies. After nooning, she worked again until nightfall, running four or five miles to each mile Julio and Pinta covered. And at night she was constantly on guard against the wolves and coyotes that yipped and howled. Julio saw no more signs of grizzly, but one morning he found the telltale tracks of a cat—a cougar or bobcat—drag marks dotted with blood, and a mother ewe who wandered about looking lost, bleating for her lamb.

Dust from hundreds of shuffling hoofs swirled with dust from the wagons. Stinging, biting flies found exposed flesh and bored through the stiff cotton shirt that Julio was now forced to wear for protection. The tormenting flies raised welts on Pinta's neck and chest, where neither she nor Julio could shoo them away. He brushed Pinta every night, rubbed medicine on her bites, and made sure she had good grass and water. But at the tail of the wagon train, he and Dick were miserable.

"Thought bein' a smithy was dirty work," Dick grumbled, wiping grit from his face with a bandanna when they stopped for nooning on the twelfth day.

"Nothing could be dirtier than this!" Julio grumbled back, reaching for the puppies.

He set the squirming blanket on the ground and pulled the edges straight. Now that the puppies' eyes were open and their little legs were growing strong, they were curious to explore the world. One, two, three, four, five. . . . "Dick! One of the puppies is missing." Julio stepped carefully into the wagon bed and finally found the yellow one way in the back, under the canvas, wedged between the salt lick and the wooden box of sheep medicine. "You wild little coyote!" he scolded. "I'll have to do something about this! If the wagon hits a bump and the load shifts, you'd get squashed back here."

"Co-*yo*-te?" Dick chuckled, taking the pup and mimicking Julio's Spanish pronunciation. "That's a fittin' name for this little mutt. There you go, Co-*yo*-te." Dick plopped the pup in the middle of the blanket with the others, and immediately Coyote's oversized paws paddled to the edge. Tail at attention, he stopped short, looked down at the ground, tipping his head from side to side, then reached out with one paw, tapped the powdery soil, and jerked away. He looked so funny Dick slapped his big hands against his legs and doubled with laughter, raising a puff of dust that made them both laugh even more.

Chivita trotted up, watching them with her head cocked first to one side, then the other as if to ask what was so funny. She sniffed her pups, then lay down on the blanket, panting. The puppies, all except for Coyote, responded to her invitation to lunch. Still laughing, Julio scooped Coyote up from the dirt and pushed him to Chivita's belly. "You're going to have to talk to this one, Chivita!" he said, stroking her head.

When the wagons began to move again, Julio emptied the contents of his basket onto the blanket, then lined the basket with the poncho and lifted the sleepy puppies into their new bed—a bed with no escape.

That afternoon and for the next several days the sun beat down, each day hotter and drier than the one before. Strange mirages rippled up from the flat plain, making antelope look like mounted ponies and crows look like attacking braves. A fierce wind came up and whipped even more dust into the already choking air. Dust and sand and grit covered Julio's skin, caked on his scalp, sifted into his ears and nose. He coughed, snorted, spit brown mucus. When he bit down, sand crunched between his teeth. At least, the wind brought some relief from mosquitoes and buffalo flies.

Last year Mr. Bent said there was rain, too much rain, Julio thought. I wish it would rain now! He was constantly thirsty, and so were the sheep. They raced out of control at the smell of water. Three sheep had already drowned, butted into the river by the sheep behind them before he and Pinta or Chivita could turn them away. He was using the skin of one old ewe as a saddle.

On and on the sheep shuffled. Through the dust, Julio could barely make out the next landmark, Point of Rocks.

To Julio it looked like a hand with an outstretched finger pointing back toward Mexico. Near Point of Rocks Julio herded the sheep toward the river, downstream from where the wagons had stopped for the night, and smelled the wet charcoal of a doused campfire. He nudged Pinta with the heels of his moccasins and rode ahead to a recently vacated campsite. The embers in the fire ring were not completely dead. A large area of trampled grass surrounded the circle. From the numbers of hoofprints and boot prints, and the quantity of chewed bones, Julio could tell that many had camped here, and the tracks told him the horses were shod, not Cheyenne ponies. There were no moccasin marks, only the imprint of boots. Just how close were they to Texas?

He trotted back to where the traders had made camp. "Mr. Bent," he said, "there's something down there I think you should see."

Bent took one last bite, set his plate aside, and mounted his white mule.

Near the river Bent rode around the trampled ground. "Warfield, I'll bet," he muttered, studying the tracks. "He and his Texans are on the prowl again."

"Lord save us from Texans!" Dick exclaimed as he walked up beside them.

"Yep." Bent nodded. "I sure pity any Mexican traders on the trail this spring. Warfield's out for plunder. He'll be robbing Mexican caravans again, raising money for their confounded bankrupt Republic."

Julio squinted his eyes and peered through the cottonwoods in the direction that Warfield's troops had gone. Warfield and his Texas freebooters were the ones who'd attacked Mora last spring, the ones who'd robbed and murdered Don Antonio Chávez the spring before, the ones my own American grandfather tried to stop.

"Don't worry too much, Julio." Bent pulled himself upright in his saddle. "The Mexican traders in Taos and Santa Fe have been warned. I sent a message from the Fort to the American consul. He'll pass the word along." Bent seemed to sink deep into his own thoughts for a moment, and when he spoke again, he sounded angry. "Julio, my Fort is a trading post, not a military fort. We stay neutral!" His voice rose, then abruptly lowered. "But when we're not neutral, we're clever. Not many Mexican traders will be going east this spring. And any Mexican traders who brave it will be escorted back to the Mexican border by American troops."

"But that's not enough!" Julio said. "What will keep Warfield from crossing into Mexico and attacking them there? At least traders carry rifles. They can try to defend themselves. But what about women and children? What will keep Warfield from attacking Mexican towns the way he did before?"

"Not a confounded thing." Bent flipped the reins, and his mule stepped out. "But they're all a bunch of bungling idiots—the Texas troops *and* the Mexican troops. They wander around starving, lost. With any luck, they'll do themselves in before they hurt anybody else."

As Bent rode away, Julio studied the tracks again. Except for two sets of prints—the two that headed east— all the others had traveled west. They could be headed to Mexico. To Taos.

Julio's thoughts spun—Texas, Mexico, the United States. Bent was American. If Bent thought Texans were crooks, the same as people in Taos thought, why would the United States admit Texas into the Union? Why would the United States fight Mexico over Texas? If they did, United States troops wouldn't be a bunch of idiots. How could we stand up to them?

Then with a jolt, Julio realized again that he was both "we" and "they." If war came, he would have to choose sides.

13

That evening, after he'd doctored the ailing sheep and spread ointment on Pinta's bites and on the wounds on his arm, Julio slumped down onto a log and sat staring into the flickering flames of the campfire. Days were getting longer, it was still light, and he'd laid stones for a fire ring under a cottonwood tree that he guessed must have been fifty or a hundred years old; its branches rustling with nesting birds. Absentmindedly he sliced off pieces of venison steak and fed them to Chivita as she lay nursing her puppies beside him.

His arm hurt from using it too much, too soon, but the claw marks had scabbed over and were beginning to itch and pull, and he knew that was a good sign. It was healing. He didn't worry about blood poisoning anymore, but he couldn't stop worrying about Warfield's troops, and what might happen to Mamá and Teresita and his other sisters, and his aunts and uncles and cousins and friends in Taos. His thoughts bounced back and forth from Spanish to English, English to Spanish, like that wooden ball on the string at the Fort.

"What's the matter, Mr. Julio?" Dick chuckled, pouring a cup of steaming coffee into his tin cup. "Looks like you carryin' the woes of the world on them shoulders."

"Ay, Dick! I'm worried about my family. What do you think will happen? The United States and Mexico going to war? Why? Last year the Americans hung two of those Texas bandits. Now American troops are protecting Mexican wagon trains from Texans. If Americans are protecting Mexicans, why would they want to go to war with Mexico? If Americans are against what Texas is doing, why would they let Texas join their country? It doesn't make sense."

"Well, I ain't no politician, Mr. Julio"—Dick paused to sip his coffee—"but the way I sees it, it don't have nothin' at all to do with sense. It has to do with aquirin' territory, and most of all, it has to do with slavery."

"Slavery!" Julio twisted sideways to look at Dick.

Dried sweat lines marked the sides of Dick's heavy cheeks, and his shirt collar was dark beneath curly twists of hair. Dick tipped his head and looked at Julio from the side of his eye. "There's rumblin' in the United States, states that wants slavery and them that don't. Texas would be another vote *for*."

"Dick! You're not . . . !"

"Yes," Dick answered slowly, focusing on a red-tailed hawk that was gliding out across the prairie. "Charlotte too. We belong to the Bent family. They sent us out here from Missouri."

Julio had to look away. He stared down at the roasting meat. What could he say? He'd heard of slaves in the United States. He'd heard that rich Mexicanos in the capital and in Chihuahua owned Indian slaves, and that some tribes stole people from other tribes to use as slaves. But Dick? Dick and Charlotte? How could William Bent own Dick and Charlotte? Weren't they all Americans? Would his grandfather own people? "Dick, it's not right! Do black people own slaves too?"

Dick's eyes watered, and his face turned a darker shade of sunburned brown. For a second, Julio thought he was having an attack, but then Dick threw his head back and bellowed a loud, long, stomach-gripping laugh that slopped coffee all over his leg.

"What's so funny over here?" Bent called out, as he rode up on his mule.

"Nothin', Mr. Bent." Dick hiccupped. "Nothin' 'cept Mr. Julio here jes' asked me the funniest question I ever heard in all mah days."

"Well, I'm glad you still have a sense of humor. Driving these sheep has got to be the worst job there is, but we've already covered about a third of the way to Independence. With luck, in another week we'll reach the Great Bend of the Arkansas and leave the river and this short grass prairie behind. Then we'll get out of the worst of the dust." Bent's mule stomped a front hoof sharply into the ground. "Julio, you've never seen anything like the country we're heading into. Once we cross Cow Creek the grass will be so high you can't see over it."

Julio turned to Dick. "Honest?"

Grinning, Dick nodded.

The mule stomped again and pulled at its reins, jerking its neck toward the river. "Next landmark out there is Pawnee Rock," Bent said, sitting easily in the saddle. "Watch for it. Sticks up like a thumb of chocolate on top of a big mound right in the middle of flat, rolling prairie. You can see it for miles."

"I 'member that place." Frowning, Dick shook his head. "You can see it for miles all right, but Kiowa or

Pawnee or Comanches or Arapahos can see *from* it for miles
too. It's jus' like a lookout tower."

"Yup." Bent nodded. "The scouts haven't seen any
signs of trouble yet, but it always pays to be watchful."
Bent turned in his saddle toward a movement along the
river. "Speaking of watchful. . . ." Bent said, lowering his
voice.

Two men rode out through the trees, ducking their
heads to avoid low branches. They weren't Mexican, Julio
could tell, but not until one of them—the big one—spoke
did Julio guess they were Americans. Or Texans.

"You William Bent?" the big one asked, his flat face
expressionless.

Bent nodded.

"We're lookin' to join up with your caravan back to
Missouri."

"Oh? Where are you boys comin' from?"

"Up along the, uh, Arkansas," the big man mumbled
through a drooping mustache. He was a stocky man in
ragged clothes. Tobacco juice and flecks of what looked
like dried egg yolk clung to his shaggy beard and down
the front of his weather-beaten shirt.

"What's your business?"

"Me and my little brother's trappers. But we're mighty
anxious to be headin' home," the big one said.

A grumbly sound came from deep in Bent's throat.
"No more anxious than I am to get my trade goods to
Missouri. What're your names?"

"Zar. My brother, Gallatin. Zar and Gallatin—uh—
Smith, from Clay County, Missouri."

"Don't recall seeing you boys out in these parts before,"
Bent said, circling the palm of his hand on the saddle horn

as if he had an itch. "Say you're trappers? Trapping along the Arkansas?"

"Yup, but we're done fed up with it. We're hankerin' for the moist air of Missouri, a mess of good fried catfish, and some real smooth whiskey. This Taos Lightning they drink out here's enough to kill a thinkin' man."

"You see signs of any Delaware?" Bent asked.

Zar only shook his head, and when he didn't answer, his little brother said in a high, soft voice, "We seen some Pawnee, didn't we, Zar? No Delaware, no sir, Mr. Bent. But we ain't starting off acrost that prairie alone. Laws!" Just at that moment he spotted Chivita and her pups. "You got yourselves some puppies." He started to kneel beside them, but his brother grabbed his sleeve and jerked him up.

"Why'd the Delaware be out so far west anyhow?" Zar grumbled.

"Same as the Pawnee most likely, picking fights with the Cheyenne and Kiowa. Counting coup. Stealing horses," Bent said, shrugging. He motioned to the flock of sheep. "Well, boys, if you're willin' to pitch in and help, I reckon you can throw in with us. Julio and Dick here could use some help. Ever drive sheep before?"

"Sheep!" Zar, the big one snorted, as if Bent had said slime or snakes.

Julio studied Bent's face, but whatever he was thinking was well hidden.

"Julio's in charge of the herd." Bent nodded his hat toward Julio. "You'll work with him. Now if you're hungry, go on up to the wagons and get your ration of meat. Julio and Dick will share their fire."

Julio glanced at Dick and knew that his face, too, masked what he thought of these new helpers. Just then several magpies broke into a raucous quarrel around their shaggy nests in the cottonwood branches overhead.

The two men rode toward the main camp, Zar in front, Gallatin trailing behind as the sun dropped like a rock behind the flat western horizon and the sky turned gray.

"Mr. Bent," Julio asked, "are those men Texans?"

Bent nailed Julio with one of his hawk looks. "You don't miss much, do you, Julio?"

"I don't know how to tell the difference. Are they Texans or Americans?"

The coldness in Bent's eyes warmed. "Ever see trappers without traps?"

Slowly Julio grinned. "No pelts either," he added. Bent ducked his head to cover a laugh. "This won't be the first time I've had Texas spies tagging along. There were at least three up at the Fort last year," he said.

"What will you do about them?" Julio watched Zar and Gallatin skirting the edge of the herd. "Aren't they dangerous?"

"There's nobody west of the Missouri that's not dangerous, Julio." The twinkle in Bent's eyes suddenly disappeared. "Never forget that. But people from Bent's Fort stay neutral. We do our best to keep peace with everyone—the tribes, the Texans, Mexico, the U.S.— everyone. And you're working for me now. Both of you." He nailed Dick with a sharp glance.

"After what Texans have done to us. . . ." Julio's thoughts again raced back to Mamá and his sisters. His hands clenched. "I can't stay neutral!"

"Listen, young man. You're entitled to any opinion you like, but as long as you work for me, you're not going to pick any fights with the Smith brothers, even if they are Texans."

Julio squared his shoulders, vowing to keep his distance from Zar and Gallatin Smith. "Mr. Bent, I don't pick fights. Not with anyone!"

The air pulsed with a strained silence until Dick broke the tension. "Don't see why they couldn't ride up there with you."

"They'll ride back here." The tone of Bent's voice left no question. "We'll have them drive the wagon. Like it or not, they stay back here. Eat here. Sleep here. Understood?"

Julio nodded.

"Mr. Bent," Dick said, looking at his feet. "I ain't riding with 'em in that wagon."

"Huh!" Bent grunted. "Well, Dick, I don't have an extra horse, but I could let you take that sheepherder's little burro. Humm." He nodded. "That's not a bad idea. Bonita's used to driving sheep."

When Zar and Gallatin returned, carrying two large hunks of dripping meat, Julio repeated Bent's instructions.

"We ain't takin' orders from no slave." Zar scowled. "Or no green-eyed Messican either."

Chivita growled low in her throat, but Julio squelched the first words that flashed into his mind. Instead, in as calm a voice as he would use with a lamb, he said, "Those aren't our orders. Mr. Bent said for you to drive the wagon. Dick and I will herd the sheep. You follow along behind."

14

Julio awoke with that wary feeling that came when danger lurked nearby. The early morning sky was still milky white, and the air was crisp. No sounds carried from the big camp. Nothing had threatened the sheep during the night. The flock was still sleeping and grazing peacefully.

Julio shook off the feeling of foreboding, folded his poncho, and tucked it with his other belongings in the wagon. He gathered dry grass and kindling and knelt to feed the coals from the cook fire. Sparks flared onto the kindling, and soon the fire burned hot. While water came to a boil, he shinnied up the cottonwood and gathered eggs from the shaggy nests of the protesting magpies, ducking their attacking beaks. He boiled coffee and mixed the eggs into flour, salt, soda, and water, fried the bread, then sprinkled it with sugar.

Even with the commotion from the magpies, Zar and Gallatin were still snoring and wheezing in their bedrolls under the tree where they had tied their horses. Horses? Julio looked again. Gallatin's mount was a roan-colored horse, but Zar's wasn't a horse at all. It was a mule, a very large brown mule, even larger than Bent's white one.

"This is mighty tasty, Mr. Julio." Dick licked sugar from his fingers. "Charlotte'd be jealous!" He rolled up his bedroll, tucked it in the wagon, and started yoking the oxen. "Reckon we ought to wake 'em up?" He nodded to Zar and Gallatin.

Julio didn't say anything, but Dick knew what he was thinking and chuckled. "At least, I don't have to ride with 'em." He slipped a piece of sugary bread between Bonita's reaching lips, then ambled over to the two snoring heaps on the ground. "Buenos dias, fellas. Breakfast's served. We're movin' out."

Neither Zar nor Gallatin talked as they gobbled their bread and downed the coffee. "Go tie Jesse and Heck to the wagon," Zar ordered. Like a scared rabbit, Gallatin jumped to his feet and fled. As he rushed past Julio, he said very softly, "That was a real tasteful breakfast. Much obliged."

Julio fit the basketful of puppies into the hollow in the wagon bed, then spread the sheepskin saddle on Pinta's back. "Ready, Pinta, for another long day?" He stroked her muzzle and down her neck, then slid onto her back. "Ovejas, Chivita. Ovejas!" he called.

"O-*bay*-hus!" Dick echoed, and another day of dust began.

"Follow along slow," Julio called to Zar. "Don't crowd the sheep." Scowling, Zar cracked the whip. "Dick, are you going to be all right on that burro?" He couldn't let himself laugh, but Bent was right. Bonita was one of the homeliest animals Julio had ever seen. Her head with its long ears was so big in proportion to her body that it looked like she might tip over frontward.

"Jes' fine, Mr. Julio. I 'spect I'll be sore, but I'm jes' fine!" Dick perched on the little burro's rump with his feet nearly dragging the ground. He tapped Bonita's shaggy coat with a thin stick. Her floppy ears swiveled, she brayed a long he-haw, shook her head, then obediently stepped forward.

It was not yet midmorning when Julio heard the rumble of the wagon wheels. He turned and watched in disbelief as Zar drove past in a wide arc around the sheep. "Zar!" he yelled, pointing back. But Zar wouldn't look at him. He drove the wagon halfway between the line of Bent's wagons and the sheep before he slowed.

"Must'a gotten their fill of dust already," Dick said, steering Bonita beside Pinta.

Julio shook his head. "*Atrevidos!* If we need something for the animals, they'd never look back." The sheep were beginning to fan out toward a gully. "Ovejas, Chivita!" Julio signaled Chivita to bring them back. "I'll talk to them."

"You be mighty careful, Mr. Julio. That Zar, he'd make three of you!"

"I know," Julio said, pulling his sling and a stone from his leather bag.

The sheep wagon was a half mile ahead of the sheep when Julio trotted up to the side of the wagon where Gallatin was riding.

"What do you need?" He leaned forward and called to Zar.

Zar scowled at him from beneath his grimy hat. "Don't need nothin', Green Eyes," he grumbled, " 'cept air."

"Good!" Julio hoped his smile didn't look too forced. "I was afraid something was wrong. You'd better take the wagon back behind the sheep, in case they need medicine. And so Chivita can get to her pups." Julio reined Pinta just enough to drop back beside the wagon bed. He leaned toward the basket and said loudly for Zar and Gallatin to hear, "Don't worry, puppies. Zar and Gallatin will take you back to your mama now." He rode away without saying anything more, thankful that his voice hadn't wobbled and that he hadn't been forced to use the sling.

By midday, the wagon was behind the flock again, but from then on, for the next several days, Zar said almost nothing to Julio and Dick. He sat like a big grumpy toad, lagging nearly a half mile behind the tail end of the wagon train. When the time came to set up camp or cook or break camp, he sat somewhere else.

As they neared Pawnee Rock scouts spotted the first braves silhouetted against the evening sky. Friendly? Hostile? They didn't know.

"Reckon we'd better stick close tonight," Zar said, stepping down from the sheep wagon.

Bent's hunter made his rounds, distributing chunks of venison from the fresh kill he'd made since nooning. Eyeing the top of Pawnee Rock, he said, "Keep a sharp lookout tonight, boys."

Julio collected buffalo chips and started the cook fire while Dick cut the venison into five steaks, mumbling in Spanish under his breath about *Los Perezosos*. Julio was the one who had started calling the Smith brothers Los Perezosos—the lazy ones—and it was true. They were the laziest men Julio had ever known. Then Dick began using the Spanish word like a secret code. That night, as always, Zar and Gallatin did nothing to help set up camp and cook.

"Chivita, ven!" Julio called Chivita away from the sheep, diverting his mind from the Smiths—and from Pawnee Rock. "You've worked hard all day. Take care of your puppies."

Panting, Chivita looked up at him with anticipation in her brown eyes. Slowly he tipped the basket onto its side, the puppies rolled out and started paddling in every direction. Chivita licked the afternoon dust from first one and then another. Then she nursed.

When the meat was ready, Zar, Gallatin, Dick, and Julio ate quickly, without talking, glancing up at the dark silhouette of rock. Suddenly Zar's fork jabbed into the last venison steak.

"That's for Chivita!" Before Julio had time to think, his knife quivered in the meat, holding it down. Zar jerked his fork away. He didn't say a word, but the look he gave Julio was deadly.

Lumbering to his feet, Zar carried his plate out of the light from their fire. Not too far, Julio was certain.

Gallatin leaned close to Julio and, in a high soft voice, whispered. "B-be careful of him, J-Julio. Zar can get real mean." Then in full voice he asked, "Do you think they'll attack?" He looked in the direction of the dark rise.

"All I know is they haven't attacked yet." Julio tied Pinta's lead rope to the wagon wheel and spread the ponchos on the ground. He placed his slingshot and a pile of stones beside the ponchos. "If they were the Apaches in the mountains above Taos, they'd sneak up on us at night to steal horses and sheep. Maybe they're Pawnee. Whoever they are, if they come, they'll probably attack the end of the wagon train first. We'll have to work together to protect the animals—and ourselves." He spoke loudly enough so Zar would hear. "I'll take the first watch."

"No, sir, Mr. Julio!" Dick was rinsing tin plates and standing them on their sides to dry. Two plates clanged together. He raised his voice. "You're plumb tuckered out. Zar, you take the first watch."

A grunt came from beyond the circle of firelight.

"Then Gallatin. Then me. Then Julio."

A lone cricket began its seesaw chirping somewhere nearby as Julio eased down onto the ground to sit beside Gallatin. He scratched beneath Chivita's ears and along her side, then set the basket upright and gathered the puppies inside.

Gallatin picked up the yellow pup. "We had an ol' yeller dog once't, back in Clay County," he said in his high, slow drawl. "Called him Coon. He was a coon dog." He rubbed Coyote's soft fur against his scruffy face.

Julio looked at Gallatin, surprised. "Clay County?" When Bent asked, that's where Zar said they were from— Clay County, Missouri. Maybe they weren't Texans after all. Maybe they weren't spies either. Julio almost laughed aloud. *Bent thinks Zar and Gallatin are spies. That's why he's put them back here herding sheep where they don't see or hear anything.*

"Nights"—Gallatin's voice dropped to a more normal pitch—"Ma used to sit in her rockin' chair and read to me and Christopher—uh, I mean Zar—and the other youngins. Ol' Coon, he'd sit at her feet and listen real hard."

"Gallatin!" Julio exclaimed. "Can you read?" He remembered Charlotte's promise—"If I learned to read, you will too, 'specially with Mr. Forester your grandpappy." Julio pulled his canvas bag toward him. "Will you teach me?"

"I don't read real good. I'm kinda slow." Gallatin hesitated. "'Sides, I don't got nothin' to teach you from." Gallatin glanced over his shoulder, scrunching down as if he were afraid Zar might jump out of the darkness and, at any moment, wallop him.

Julio reached into the bag. "Teach me from this."

"A Bible?" For a moment Gallatin's eyes went fuzzy, and he gazed deep into the flickering flames. "The Good Book. That's what Ma read from too." He set the yellow pup back on the ground by the basket and took the Bible. Holding it gently, he let his fingers trace over the soft leather cover and gold lettering. Julio glanced at Dick, who'd finished cleaning up and was stretching out on his bedroll beside them.

Gallatin opened the book, somewhere toward the end, and trailed his finger beneath the words as he read slowly, "Bless-ed are the pure in heart, for they shall see God."

The punk wood in the fire smoked and sizzled, then flamed up, lighting Gallatin's features. He sat still, so still he hardly seemed to breathe. Then in a near whisper, almost as if he were half asleep, Gallatin said, "Me and my brother done a terrible thing."

The cricket stopped chirping. A footstep crunched behind them, and Gallatin's breath sucked in fast. "But that was two years ago, before Owl—before what happened—and we ain't done nothin' bad since," he said, quickly turning the pages back to the beginning. He glanced down, then twisted toward the firelight, studying the smeared words on the page.

"These your folks?" He pointed to the handwriting, sounding out the name at the top, "My-ron For-es-ter." His finger stopped, quivered. "Myron Forester!"

"That's my grandfather. Do you know him?"

"No!" Gallatin's voice creaked. "N-never heard of nobody called Myron Forester." Thrusting the Bible back into Julio's hands, he scrambled to his feet, tripped over Dick's legs, and stumbled out of the light.

The next morning Julio was not surprised to see Gallatin's blackened eye. He had heard the brief scuffle and harsh, whispered words in the middle of the night.

15

During that night no attack came. Nor did it come the next day or the next night. Pawnee Rock sank into the prairie still hiding silhouettes and shadows. Now, day after day, the wagon and sheep moved eastward, trailing the wagon train. Little by little, the grama grass became thicker. In the mornings buffalo grass sparkled with dew, and in the distance great herds of buffalo looked like moving groves of trees.

The sheep developed thrush, coughs, flux. Sheepskins piled onto the sheep wagon, drawing flies as they cured. The flock fell farther and farther behind, and the farther they fell behind the more threatening the occasional silhouettes on the horizon became. Now Zar and Gallatin kept the wagon close to the sheep.

Gallatin avoided Julio. If he had to answer a question, he used grunts or single words and never looked into Julio's eyes. When they stopped, Zar paced like a trapped animal, watching for signs of smoke or silhouettes, then looking off toward the northeast, always looking northeast. With each day that passed, tension drew tighter and tighter like a taut bowstring.

"Look at Los Perezosos!" Dick's scrawny burro, Bonita, plodded at Pinta's side with Dick sitting astride her rump.

Dick jerked his chin at the sheep wagon, and Bonita flopped her fuzzy ears.

As always, both Zar and Gallatin were riding in the wagon, Heck and Jesse tied behind. They didn't chase after stray sheep, they didn't help skin the dead ones, they didn't hunt, they didn't gather wood or buffalo chips for the fire, they didn't cook. Other than taking care of their own animals, they didn't do anything but sit and ride, eat and sleep, and Zar grumbled constantly. After the night of the black eye, Gallatin had not talked to Julio again—not about Clay County or reading or anything else.

Now, far up the trail, Julio saw a rider backtracking from the main wagon train. The sheep wagon stopped. Quickly Zar jumped down, mounted his horse, and galloped to the far flank of the herd, sending the sheep into a panic.

"Now he's pretendin' to work!" Dick muttered, sliding off Bonita's rump. In a streak of black and white, Chivita dashed after the fleeing sheep, herding them back to the center.

William Bent bore down on Julio and Dick. "You're falling behind! Keep these sheep moving!"

"We're doing our best, Mr. Bent," Julio said, pulling the bandanna from his face. "Dick and I are."

"Your best isn't good enough!" Bent's hat nodded toward a low ridge where the dark figures were outlined against a low bank of white fluffy clouds. "Our visitors up there have been waiting for a chance like this ever since Pawnee Rock. You have to keep up!"

"But Mr. Bent, so many lambs are lame! They keep coming down with—"

"Move 'em! Leave the sick ones. Catch up!" Bent clucked to his mule, circled, and rode away.

Julio looked after Bent, then down at a ewe that was collapsing onto her knees, breathing heavily. She bleated and a lamb with a long drooping tail dropped at her side. They were tired, depleted. All the sheep were worn out. No wonder so many were getting sick. "But we've got to keep moving," Julio said, gently laying the lamb across Pinta's shoulders and prodding the ewe with his staff. "Or you'll never get to Bent's farm, and I'll never get to my grandfather in time."

In time. Beneath the surface, that phrase had gnawed at him since he left Bent's Fort. Charlotte and Dick said my grandfather planned to search for us for ten years. Julio thought, if I was three or four years old then, and I'm fifteen now, ten years could be over.

In time. Julio and Dick plodded along at the sheep's pace. The slow life of a shepherd had never bothered him before, but now that his arm was healing, now that questions and decisions tugged at him from so many directions, this pace seemed deadly. He wanted to break loose, wanted to yell, "Hurry up! Hurry up! Let's go!"

Now Julio watched, expecting exactly what happened. As soon as Bent was out of sight, Zar hitched his horse to the wagon again and climbed back onto the seat. He took the reins from Gallatin, snapped the bullwhip, and the oxen lumbered ahead.

"I'm not cookin' for Los Perezosos!" Dick said, slapping his sombrero against his leg. "No more! I ain't *their* slave."

Julio had never seen Dick lose patience before. Bonita's ears pivoted, but she didn't miss a step.

"If they don't do their share of the work, they don't eat!"

"Tonight nobody eats," Julio said, calculating the distance they would have to cover to close the gap between them and the wagons. "Tonight we'll drive these poor animals until they drop or until we catch up."

"Now look at 'em!" Dick shook the sombrero at the Smiths. "What are they doin'?"

Zar was whipping the oxen. Harder and harder he drove them, jouncing the wagon mercilessly over the deep ruts, jerking Heck's and Jesse's lead ropes.

"Slow down!" Julio shouted. "Chivita's puppies are back there!" But he knew Zar couldn't hear him.

Zar rumbled past the sheep. "They're leaving us behind! They're heading straight through that buffalo wallow, going up with the other wagons." But just as Julio shouted, a loud crack like a rifle shot snapped the air. The wagon jerked lamely to one side and lurched to a stop behind the staggering oxen.

"They broke a wheel!" Dick exclaimed.

But Julio wasn't looking at the wheel. He was looking at the reason Zar had taken off so quickly. Three braves were trotting down a slope toward them—different braves, he thought, from the ones who'd been trailing the wagons. What would happen if they weren't friendly? For a second, before he urged Pinta forward, the word "Protector" echoed through his mind.

Sombrero still in hand, Dick slid from Bonita's rump. "Be careful, Mr. Julio."

Julio rode through the flock directly toward the braves. With heavily loaded panniers, leather boxes, weighing down their ponies, they did not look like a war party. Maybe they wanted to trade. Julio slowed and was just raising his hand in greeting when he heard Zar's shouts.

"Go back!" Zar yelled, slashing his arm downward. "Get out of here!" He rushed to the back of the wagon bed, stumbled, kicked something out of his way, and tried to mount his mule, but Jesse pranced and would not let him near. "I'm warning you Injuns! Get away!" Zar waved again, his hand, palm down.

The braves slowed, studying Julio, then Zar, and urged their ponies on faster toward the older man.

"No!" Julio cried out, kicking Pinta's sides. "Zar, no!"

But Zar was raising his rifle.

"Don't shoot! You signaled them to come!" Julio shouted, but it was too late. Zar's rifle blazed. One of the braves jerked backward with the impact of the bullet. He righted himself, clutching his left arm. Then the three turned and galloped back up the rise.

"Don't! Don't shoot again!" Julio leaped from Pinta's back, grabbing the hot barrel of Zar's Hawkins.

"Why, you little—" The back of Zar's hand sliced toward Julio's face.

Julio's knife was faster. He leveled the blade right where Zar's blow was aimed.

Zar checked his swing just in time. He stepped back, scowling.

Julio didn't move.

"I warned 'em to get away," Zar grumbled.

"You signaled them to come!" Still holding the knife blade flat, Julio repeated Zar's signal, palm downward, the way Zar had done. "Don't you know? This sign means *come. Hurry!* You told them to come, to hurry! Then you shot at them!"

"Well, they're hurryin' now." Zar spit a long brown stream of tobacco juice. "Back to where they belong. They was makin' me nervous followin' us like that."

Julio was too angry for caution. "They're not even the same braves who were following us before!" Julio stopped, took a deep breath, and lowered his voice. "They won't go away and forget this. They'll be back. Maybe tonight, maybe tomorrow, maybe longer. But they'll be back. You've wounded one and insulted their tribe."

Julio rammed his knife back into the sheath and swung himself up onto Pinta's back. "Dick and I are driving sheep tonight. Catch up when that wheel is fixed. We won't wait for you." He steered Pinta to the back of the wagon bed and quickly untied Jesse and Hank's lead ropes. "I'll take care of your animals for you until you catch up." And, he thought, to guarantee that you won't ride off and abandon the wagon.

Zar's nostrils flared. "Why, you—!" His eyes narrowed as he scanned the horizon, then he hunkered down beside the wheel. "Gallatin!" he bellowed. "Git down here'n help me with this. Bring your rifle."

Gallatin scooted across the wagon seat and climbed down on the opposite side. For a moment, he stooped out of sight. When he stood again, cuddled against his chest was the limp body of Chivita's yellow pup.

"Ya didn't have ta kick it, Zar." Tears pooled in Gallatin's eyes. "Ya didn't have ta kill it."

Blinking hard, clamping his teeth together, Julio tugged at Jesse and Heck's lead ropes, nudged Pinta to the wagon, grabbed the basket of puppies, and galloped away.

16

Julio and Dick drove the sheep deep into the night. Astride Pinta, Julio carried the five surviving puppies in the basket on his back, the basket Silent Walker made for him when he and Dancing Feather trapped eagles. Silent Walker . . . Dancing Feather . . . Papá . . . Teresita . . . Memories pulsed to the beat of Pinta's hoofs. Coyotes yipped high piercing cries that trailed off to silence. Julio's head nodded forward, and he battled to keep his eyes open.

He slipped the flute from his leather bag and played as he rode, music to calm the sheep, music to calm the fear that rode beneath his ribs. But it was difficult not to remember the horror of the night when he and Papá were attacked by Apaches.

Clouds billowed higher and higher around the horizon, covering the stars and the last trace of starlight. Animals dropped and strayed. Chivita's head hung low. Her feet scraped the ground; she was exhausted. Finally it was too dark, too dangerous to go on.

Julio felt in his canvas bag for the matches. "I've been saving these for a time we really needed them, Dick," he said. "I think that's now." He opened the little box, took out a strip of flat wooden matches, and broke off the first match. On the second strike, it flamed. As tired as he was, Julio stared in awe. What magic could make fire leap on the end of a stick of wood? He'd heard the Americans call the matches Lucifers. Had they tapped the magic of an evil power?

Julio and Dick had no hot dinner. As soon as the small fire caught, Julio pulled out a piece of flaming wood for a torch. "You sleep, Dick," he said. "Chivita and I will take first watch." Dick nodded and crumpled onto the bare ground, already asleep, curled into a ball on his side beside the basket of sleeping pups.

Slowly Julio and Chivita circled the flock, guiding the sheep into a tight circle as they turned from the light of Julio's torch. Once, twice, three times they circled around. Sheep bleated and grunted; lambs cried. Julio tried not to think about the lambs they'd left for coyotes and magpies and buzzards. Too many to skin. Their small pelts weren't worth the time it would have taken.

When the torch lost its flame, Julio sat on the ground. It was pitch dark. Not a single star peeked through the clouds. He listened, but there were no suspicious sounds. The back of his neck didn't prickle with warning. The night was too dark even for Pawnee to attack. Julio felt in the leather bag at his side and again pulled out his flute. He licked his lips that were dry and chalky with dust, then began to play.

How many times, how many places had he played this flute since the day Papá had given him the piece of hollow reed? I had just begun watching the sheep at night, Julio remembered. I was about seven years old, and I've played this flute ever since. As his music spread over the tired flock, that day with Papá again came alive in his memory. "A man from the Bay of Banderas came through Taos," Papá had said. "I traded him a block of Tia Inez's goat cheese for this bamboo. It's for you. And for the sheep. They will like it."

"To eat?" Julio had asked, and Papá laughed.

"No. It's for a flute. Bamboo grows this way, already hollow. Leave this end closed." Papá ran his thumb over the end where a new segment of bamboo had grown. "Then carve holes—one to blow into and as many as you want for your fingers."

Julio remembered his joy at the gift, the care he'd taken in planning and carving the holes. He didn't know where the fingers should go to make the best sounds, so he held the bamboo between his fingers and thumbs and with a piece of charcoal marked the place each finger pad touched. He carved a smooth round hole for each finger. The first time he played, Papá's eyes had glowed with pride. The last time he played, Silent Walker's eyes had smiled. Her look of fear came later when he hadn't taken the feathers.

Little by little the lingering complaints of the sheep died, and the whole mass of dusty, smelly wool breathed its way into sleep.

The lament of Julio's flute droned on, keeping him awake. The notes sang of things past—Teresita, Papá, Dancing Feather, Silent Walker, and the tune from the woman in his vision who called him Billy.

> I gave my love a cherry
> Without no stone—

My grandfather knows this song! Julio was suddenly wide awake.

Later Dick stood guard while Julio slept, but it seemed like only minutes before he heard, "Mr. Julio?" and Dick was nudging his leg with his foot. "Your watch."

"I was dreaming, Dick." Julio sat up and shook his head, still in another world, blinking from the brightness of Dick's torch. "I dreamed about Teresita. She was weaving something . . . something big, like a shawl from wool she'd spun from Tia Inez's best angora goats. There were three colors—purple, green, and blue. She was sitting in tall grass, weaving those colors together and singing." He shook his head. "I miss the way Teresita always sings."

"Cain't say I miss the way Charlotte sings." Groaning, Dick eased himself onto the ground.

"But Dick, the dream was so real. Teresita, singing and singing, and then a bear rose up from the grass and I was running, trying to get to her, but I wasn't moving. Couldn't move. I was running, but I wasn't getting any closer. Then, then an old man walked into the meadow. He was very calm. He picked up the shawl Teresita was making and tossed it over the bear and the bear disappeared."

"Disappeared?"

"Yes." Julio sighed. "Poof, just like that! What do you think it means?"

Dick handed over the torch. "I couldn't rightly say, Mr. Julio. But maybe it means it's *my* turn to dream."

The morning was muggy and clouds hung heavy over the land. Dew flattened the sheep's wool, grimy brown on top, white in the valleys. Behind the herd, the sheep wagon was nowhere in sight. Ahead there was no sign of the wagon train.

For breakfast, Julio and Dick ate only dried biscuits and drank water. "We've got to catch up to the wagons this morning," Julio said. "If there's trouble coming from those Pawnee—or whoever they are—the weather may have saved us last night."

Dick swatted dew from his sombrero. "Yes," he agreed, but Chivita looked up with sad eyes, whining.

"What's the matter, girl?" Julio knelt beside her.

Chivita nosed the puppies and whined once again.

Julio groaned. The puppies were tottering and tumbling outside the basket, exploring their rutted world. But there were only four. One was missing. He looked around, checking the ground for tracks—coyote, wolf, fox—but there were no tracks except for Bonita's and Pinta's and the sheep. In that black night, anything could have sneaked in while he and Chivita were working the sheep and Dick was dead asleep—or the other way around. "I'm sorry, Chivita," he said, touching his forehead to hers, holding her head between his hands. "It was a black-and-white one like you."

"Maybe an owl." Dick looked up at the gray sky.

Julio shivered. An owl, a silent evil who could see in the dark, a messenger of death. A bad omen.

Julio and Dick were yelling and prodding the sheep to move when the sheep wagon rumbled slowly into view again. The weather had protected Los Perezosos from the Pawnee too. In spite of himself, Julio breathed a sigh of relief, but he did not go to greet Zar and Gallatin. He merely waved as they rolled slowly by.

"Ahead of us," Julio said.

"Uh-huh," Dick grunted.

By midmorning, a fine mist filled the air. Except for tickling Julio's nose and face, it was hardly there. The mist was warm, not like the sharp cold raindrops back in the West, each drop like an icy spear not to be ignored. Moisture collected and balanced on the tips of grass so tall that they reached above his stirrups. The grass here was much taller, thicker than he'd seen before, and there were many more kinds of trees, some with black bark. Julio breathed deeply, glad for the fresh air washed clean of dust. Even the sheep seemed more content.

Strange hollow sounds, creaking sounds, and dongs like muffled cowbells wafted through the fog. Ahead dark shapes emerged from the mist. Julio blinked, then recognized the nodding heads of two enormous bulls and the white covering of a wagon. Off to one side, more bulls, more wagons slid from the fog. It was a wagon train, westward bound.

Abruptly the sheep wagon stopped. Zar and Gallatin rushed to Heck and Jesse, throwing on saddles and saddlebags. Zar rode only close enough to Julio to be within earshot. "Whole bunch of sheep got away from you during the night. Ran that way. Gallatin and me 're going back after 'em." Zar rejoined Gallatin, and they rode off the trail, quickly disappearing from sight.

Dick snorted. "Stray sheep! Them sheep didn't stray nowhere durin' the night! They was too tuckered out."

"I don't think they did either," Julio agreed, but it had been dark. He and Dick had been herding blind. "But we might not have seen them."

"Even if we didn't see them, Chivita would have known. Ask me, Los Perezosos are the runaways. They're hidin' from somethin' or from someone." Dick flipped the sombrero off his head. "Maybe them braves will find 'em and fix 'em good."

The wagons continued to creak by half hidden in the mist, the drivers silent gray ghosts nodding and waving. A voice cut through the fog, and Bent's horse veered away from the westbound wagons. "Good luck to you too," Bent called. "Thanks for the warning, and watch out for Pawnee."

"Mr. Bent," Julio urged Pinta toward him. "We drove the sheep late, but the clouds . . . it was too dark. We had to stop."

Bent glanced at the abandoned sheep wagon. "I know, Julio." He sighed. "Mornin' Dick. What happened here? Where are our spies?" He dismounted and ran his hand over the rawhide wrapped wheel. Julio was surprised to see that the Smiths had done an excellent job of repairing the break.

Dick smashed his sombrero over his hair. "They *say* they're lookin' for stray sheep."

"More than likely they joined those wagons and turned back west," Bent grumbled. "Confounded spies! Found out the news they wanted to know from folks on these passing wagons and headed back to Warfield and his Texas freebooters."

"But they didn't talk with anybody." Julio was certain. "We'd have seen them."

"Maybe not," Bent said. "But by now they've circled back and found out the same thing I did. Back in March—March 1, to be exact—before President Tyler left office, he signed the papers to admit Texas into the Union. And now this new United States president, Polk, wants the lands of California and Oregon too. The whole country seems to believe that the United States has some divine right to expand from sea to sea. Manifest Destiny, they call it. Polk has already sent out troops and expeditions. He doesn't acknowledge it publicly, but now there will be a war with Mexico for sure."

War? For sure? Julio's heart skipped. Again doubts assaulted him. *I should turn back. Head home with that westbound caravan. How can I be American if Americans fight against my family? But how could I leave Dick alone with all these sheep? And I promised Mr. Bent. . . .*

"Well, the Smiths—or whatever their names are—ought to be real happy," Bent said. "It's just what they wanted." His nostrils flared and he slumped in his saddle, silently staring into the fog. The coarse bleat of an old ewe seemed to pull Bent from his thoughts. He looked down at the ewe. "Can you manage without those two?"

"Manage without them!" Julio laughed. "Mr. Bent, the Smith brothers never did anything to help—except drive the wagon and fix that wheel, and it was Zar's fault it broke."

"I don't think they turned back." Dick peered into the wagon. "They didn't take all their gear. I reckon they're hidin' from something or lookin' for somethin'." He frowned. "You know," he said, running his hand down over Bonita's fuzzy ear. "That makes me remember one night I heard 'em talkin' and Zar said somethin' about goin' back to Owl Creek to get it. Ain't we comin' up on Owl Creek, Mr. Bent?"

"Owl Creek! Get what?" Bent stiffened. "Owl Creek's where—You don't suppose—"

Owl? A shiver raced across Julio's shoulders. Owl Creek? Was this a second bad sign? First the puppy, now a creek? Julio thought Bent was going to say something more about Owl Creek, but instead he said, "Then it's a good thing they've gone!"

Dick shrugged. "I reckon they'll be comin' back."

Bent's lips clamped together. His eyes seemed to sink more deeply into his head. "They won't be back."

How could Bent be so sure? Julio glanced into the wagon bed. Dick was right. Zar's and Gallatin's bedrolls were still there. "But Zar and—"

"They won't be back," Bent repeated firmly. "Now listen. There's no time to waste. Owl Creek crosses the trail a couple of miles that way. Usually it's something you could spit across, just a shallow brush creek. But that wagon master said the creek's rising fast from runoff. When this storm cracks open, we could be in real trouble. If the weather stays bad, the Little Arkansas Crossing will be even worse." Bent slipped his hat from his head and looked out across the dawdling herd.

"I know you're doing all you can to keep these sheep moving, but I have to push hard now. Real hard. Cross the wagons before dark while the animals are broken in. Don't dare wait till morning. I just can't risk a crossing like that with animals cold to the harness. They'd be too hard to control."

Dick nodded. "That's right, Mr. Bent. You best keep going."

Bent shook his head. "I don't have any choice."

"It's all right," Julio said, but he thought he must be crazy to say it was all right to be left with hundreds of sheep and only two men and one sheep dog on the opposite side of a rising river. Especially with a Pawnee threat and a storm moving in.

"Julio," Bent said, looking off through the fog. "You're doing a good job, a real good job, more than herding sheep. I've seen the way you get along—with the Cheyenne, the Mexicans, folks at the Fort, even the Smith brothers. You're like your papá—and your grandfather too—a peacemaker." Bent wiped his hand across his face and for a moment looked down. "We're over halfway to the farm. It's another two hundred and forty miles, more or less, but I want to say this now." He looked directly into Julio's eyes. "I don't know what you'll find in Independence. Don't know if your grandpa'll be there. Don't know if you'll fit into his way of living if he is there. But if things don't work out, I'd be glad to have you sign on with me at Bent's Fort. The West needs men like you."

For a few seconds, Julio couldn't find any words to say in response. Finally he simply said, "Thank you."

Bent waved his thanks away. "Any more signs of our friends?" Bent nodded toward the northwest.

"Ay, Dios!" Julio exclaimed. "I should have told you right away! Three braves rode down yesterday. Zar shot one. I'm almost sure they wanted to trade. Their panniers were full."

"What!" Bent shouted. "Shot one!" He rammed the palm of his hand against the wagon bed. "Dead?"

"Wounded."

"That fool! Texas is in. The United States is going to war with Mexico. Creek's rising. Storm's building. Sheep are lagging. And now we'll have the whole Pawnee nation down on us." Bent spun away from Julio and Dick, gripped the rough, splintered wood of the wagon bed, and shook it so hard the wagon creaked.

Julio glanced at Dick, but he didn't seem concerned about Bent. He was peering through the fog in the direction the Smiths had gone.

Bent pushed away from the wagon and turned, slump-shouldered. "All right," he said in a dull, flat voice. "That changes everything. If the Pawnee make any surprise moves, take off. Catch up with the wagons. Cross Owl Creek tonight."

"We couldn't just leave the sheep!"

"If you have to, leave the sheep! I'd rather lose sheep than men."

17

The early morning fog lifted, but the sky did not lighten. Dark, packed clouds flattened out above the sheep like sheets of metal, and raw energy coursed through the clouds, twisting and sculpting snarling gray shapes overhead.

"Easy there," Julio said softly. "This will make it better." He held a wounded ewe between his knees while her lamb stood by, bleating. A wolf's or coyote's tooth may have punctured the ewe's forehead, just above her nose, or she may have run into a sharp limb. Whatever had caused it, the wound had abscessed, and the abscess was as large as Julio's fist, stretched tight with pus. If it wasn't lanced, the way Papá had taught him, she—and then her lamb—would die.

Julio wiped the blade of his knife on the dewy grass. The ewe's eyes were rolling up into her forehead. She blinked, struggled to get up, but her head dropped, and her eyes rolled up again until only the whites showed. *"Pobre oveja,"* he said, lapsing into the language he'd always spoken with sheep, Papá's way. "Poor sheep. You're almost dead." The ewe didn't protest even to the rumble of distant thunder.

With one hand, Julio pressed down to hold her head still. With the other, he eased the point of his blade through the sparse wool over the abscess and through the first layer of skin. Instantly, putrid, bloody pus spewed a long stream of vile-smelling liquid right into his face. Gagging, Julio spun away.

When his heaves subsided, Julio wiped his face with wet prairie grass. Holding his breath, he took the ewe's head again, alternately pressing out pus and dry heaving from the stench until the wound emptied. He swabbed thick homemade yellow ointment over the cut.

The ewe's brown-green eyes rolled back down where they belonged. She looked at him blankly, shook her head, flipping ointment, and crawled onto her knees. Bleating to her lamb, she stumbled back toward the flock.

Julio laughed. "Tough old mama, aren't you? I'll check on you again tomorrow. With that yellow face, you won't be hard to find." He stored the ointment in the medicine box in the wagon bed next to Zar's and Gallatin's bedrolls and the hundred pounds of salt that remained for the sheep to lick.

In spite of Bent's certainty, Julio still expected the Smith brothers to return. Why would they leave without taking their bedrolls? But now that the last of the sheep had passed the deserted sheep wagon, and the westward wagon train had disappeared into the mist, he decided Bent must have been right. Zar and Gallatin had headed west. Back to Texas. Good riddance, Julio thought, except that now Dick and I will have to take turns driving the wagon and only one of us can be with the flock.

He tied Pinta behind the wagon and threw her sheepskin saddle into the wagon bed. "Come on, puppies. Time to go again." Chivita's puppies were bouncing and tumbling, biting each other, chasing and pouncing. Julio reached for one, then another, but they scampered away as if they knew what lay ahead, as if they were saying, We're tired of riding in that wagon. With a yip, the solid black one pointed its nose and darted under the wagon bed and back out again on the other side, yipping and running as fast as its little paws could carry it.

"You little bandido! You come back here!" Finally, catching him, he secured Chivita's puppies in the wagon bed and climbed onto the seat behind the oxen. "Vamos," he said, snapping the whip near their ears.

In the distance, muffled thunder rumbled, then rolled closer and louder overhead, thumping like a broken wagon wheel. A second clap of thunder sounded even closer. Then a third exploded full force, directly overhead. It was the loudest, closest thunder Julio had ever heard, vibrating through the wooden wagon floor, into his bones, through his teeth. "Santa María!" he exclaimed, pulling on the reins to keep the oxen in check, glancing back to check on the puppies.

The wave of sound rumbled into the distance, and so did the sheep. Terrified sheep scampered in every direction, a group here, another group there. A large bunch was running as fast as they could back toward the west. Lightning flashed high, layered in the clouds, spurring them on even faster, farther.

"Dick!" Julio waved.

"Ain't no use," Dick said, letting the stick he used to guide Bonita dangle from his hand. "They're spooked. They'll run a mile that way, another mile *that* way." He waved his arm as if he were throwing a lariat. "Take us a half day to get 'em together again."

"And Bent wants us to catch up!" Julio kept a firm hold on the oxen. "Easy, easy," he kept his voice level. Even the even-tempered oxen were uneasy.

Before Dick could respond, another jolt thundered overhead. Lightning slashed down from the clouds, cracking and splintering. Julio's arms tingled. The air turned deep blue. A strange smell surrounded them, and lightning seared a trail from the back of one sheep to another to another, leaving a line of dead, smoking carcasses in its wake. Then, as if the lightning had ripped opened the bottom of the sky, rain gushed down. There were no raindrops. A river of rain pounded down, so thick Julio could scarcely breathe.

"Lord help us!" Dick crawled out from under the wagon. "We're mighty lucky, Mr. Julio. That was too close."

Looking from the sopping carnage to the fleeing sheep, Julio did not feel lucky at all. More terrified now than ever, the remaining sheep had separated on either side of the lightning line. Half of them were racing at breakneck speed in the direction of Owl Creek.

Julio tied the reins to the brake handle and slid down from the wagon seat. "I have to stop them, Dick," he yelled. "Owl Creek is over that way. Bent said it angles in until it crosses the trail. Those sheep will tumble right into it if I don't head them off."

Hastily Julio saddled Pinta and untied her reins from the wagon bed. She was jumpy, but calmed when he ran his hand down her wet neck and talked softly into her ear. "It's all right now, Pinta. It's all right now—I hope. But it's a miracle the lightning didn't hit *us* too."

Pinta rubbed her wet muzzle against his sleeve, and he flinched. His arm was much better, but it was still tender.

As if she, too, needed reassurance, Chivita came panting to his side, so wet she looked half her usual size. Dripping, she stood in front of him and looked deeply into his eyes. He knelt. "Just do the best you can, Chivita," he said. "That's all we can do now. Save as many sheep as we can."

In the cluster of sheep Chivita had managed to keep together, Julio spotted a ewe ready to bolt. *Bring her back,* Julio signaled, and Chivita, a soggy wet mat of black and white, zigzagged like the lightning, jumping from the back of one sheep to the back of another, then another, through the pounding rain until she reached the straying leader.

Julio nudged Pinta into a gallop around the other runaways, rain running down his neck, soaking into his sheepskin saddle. How could tired sheep run so far, so fast? Pinta finally overtook the wild-eyed sheep in the lead. At the tree-lined edge of the Owl Creek, she circled in front of the stampeding herd, turning them like a swirling wave away from the steep, muddy bank and the snarling water below.

Julio reined Pinta in. Chivita raced toward him, soaked ears flying. "Let's take them back, Chivita!" he said, signaling. "Good work, Pinta." Breathing hard, Pinta shook her head, flipping rain, and nickered. Then suddenly she stiffened. Her head jerked to the left, and her ears pricked forward. Now Julio heard the sound too—other horses, answering her. Pawnee? Ay, Dios! Not now! Please!

Julio leaned closer to Pinta's back. He slipped down, crouched low, and crept through the thick bushes that grew among the trees on the edge of the creek. Through the rain, he could make out four blurry figures. The two large animals were not Indian ponies, and the two men were not Pawnee.

Zar and Gallatin hadn't headed back to Texas after all. But what were they doing down there? One of them was on the ground in the mud. The other was standing over him. Was someone hurt? What had happened?

Bent said he didn't want to risk men's lives. Julio wasn't sure Bent meant these men, but he had to help if he could.

Another tremendous clap of thunder exploded overhead. Pinta started. "Easy, girl. Easy. I'll be right back." Julio looped the reins loosely over a dripping bush, and slipping-sliding in the mud climbed down toward the brown murky water that roiled in the usually shallow bed of Owl Creek.

Jesse brayed as Julio drew near. "Gallatin! Zar!" Julio called out. "What happened? Are you all right?"

The first time he called they didn't hear him over the tumbling water and rumbling sky. "Zar! Gallatin!" A log rolled under his feet and splashed into the water as he slid down the bank. "Do you need help?"

Zar wheeled around. His hand reached for his gun. "What the—!"

Gallatin leaped to his feet, sliding in mud. In one hand, he was holding a short-handled shovel, in the other, a block of brown, muddy leather.

"Are you hurt?" Julio asked again, regaining his balance, but he could see now that they were all right. No one was wounded. And he could see that even though Zar recognized him, his gun didn't drop.

Zar motioned with the gun for Julio to come forward. "Thought we was done with you, Green Eyes. Too bad you didn't stay with them stinkin' sheep"—he cocked the trigger—"where you belong."

"Zar," Gallatin whimpered, "what ya gonna do?"

Zar glared at Gallatin. "Well, what do you think?"

The hair on the back of Julio's neck stiffened. He glanced up through the trees in the wild hope Dick or Chivita would be there, but no one was. He couldn't even see Pinta. "What's this about?" Julio asked, trying to keep his voice light, friendly.

"Don't play dumb, Green Eyes. You know what this is."

Julio looked through the rain to where Zar looked, to the stack of mud-covered leather bars. He'd seen leather-wrapped bullion—gold bullion—before in the Taos plaza being unloaded from wagons. Owl Creek! Suddenly his memory linked the names. Owl Creek—Chávez! Owl Creek was where Don Antonio was robbed. He glanced at the bar in Gallatin's hand and knew without a doubt it had belonged to Don Antonio José Chávez. Julio shuddered. Zar and Gallatin were murderers!

Zar leveled the gun. "Turn around!"

Julio's heart pounded. Over the thunder, Dick would never hear the shot. Nobody would find his body; nobody would ever know what happened to him. He would never meet his grandfather or see Teresita or Silent Walker or Chivita ever again. Without closing his eyes, he prayed. Santa María, he prayed. Please! Please, don't let me come this far to die here like Don Antonio, shot down and left for the coyotes.

"I said turn around!"

Julio's muscles tightened. He stared at the dark hole in Zar's gun, but he didn't turn. He made himself breathe. Then he forced his eyes to look away from the gun and at Gallatin. "Gallatin?" He held him in his line of vision. Rain trickled down Julio's eyebrow, down his cheek beside his eye, but he did not blink.

Abruptly Gallatin threw the shovel and gold bullion into the mud. "No, Zar!" He swept his rifle from the saddle, cocked it, and aimed it at his brother. "We never intended to kill nobody. Never. Not from the beginnin'. We ain't killers. It was McDaniel not us, that pulled the trigger first. That wasn't what we set out to do. We was gonna rob Mexican wagons. That's all, and for good reason. Last time I didn't do nothing to stop the murderin', but I ain't gonna stand for it again." The rifle trembled in Gallatin's hands, and the words wobbled from his mouth as if they'd been waiting for years to be spoken. "I ain't gonna' let you do it either, Zar. It ain't right. Like Ma read us from the Good Book. The robbin' was justified, but we ain't gonna be murderers."

Zar snorted. "You wanna go home to Ma with this gold, or you wanna go back to Texas? We sure cain't go nowhere near to Independence draggin' along a grandson of that meddlin' old man Forester, now can we? They'd slap us in jail 'fore we even saw Ma. Or worse. Hang us like they hanged McDaniel and Brown."

"They was the leaders, Zar. They didn't hang the other fellas. They wouldn't us neither, unless we killed someone else." Gallatin's rifle raised again. "So we ain't gonna' kill Julio. Let's just tie him up and leave him here."

Zar hawked, spit, then wiped his nose on the back of his gun hand. "Bullet'd be more merciful." He shrugged.

"But have it your way. It'll amount to the same thing." Zar reached for the rope looped around his wet saddle horn. Gun leveled, he walked toward Julio. "Turn around!"

This time Julio turned. Zar's hand landed hard in the middle of his back, and Julio sprawled, face down in mud, rain beating against the back of his head.

"You want to know why I hate you Messicans—and Messican-lovers—so much?" Zar jerked the rope around Julio's wrists and yanked it tight. "Because of what you done to us Texas soldiers." He tugged the rope even tighter, burning Julio's skin. "We was starving, dying of thirst. We'd been lost, wandering in the wilderness. Stumbled into Santa Fe, asking for help, and you!" He yanked the rope around Julio's ankles, jerking his legs to his wrists, looped and pulled the rope tight. "You Messicans forced us to march all the way from Santa Fe to Mexico City. Treated us worse than dogs. Took everything we had, locked us in prisons. Rats and vermin crawlin' all over!" With each explosion of words, he pulled the ropes tighter. "Way I see it, Green Eyes, when we took this gold, we was only stealing back what was rightful ours—what you Messicans stole from us."

You Messicans! Julio clenched his fists tight, clenched every muscle in his body as tightly as he could. He filled his chest with air, pressing back against the ropes, hoping to create slack while his mind pressed back the words that threatened to spring from his tongue. Don't say it! Don't say anything! Nothing I say will help now.

He relaxed his fists and twisted his wrists. Jute chewed his skin, but the rope held no slack, and he realized he could no more stop what was happening to him than he could stop the thunder from rumbling overhead.

18

Zar yanked Julio into a half-sitting position against a tree. He jerked the rope around his chest and the tree trunk, then knotted the rope behind him. The scars from the grizzly wounds threatened to split open. Warmth trickled from rope burns, mixed with the cold rain, and ran down his arm, and the knotted gag Zar forced into his mouth nearly made him vomit.

"Cover him up." Zar snagged a branch from the rushing stream. " 'Case somebody comes along. They spotted Chavez too easy, what was left of him." The branch whacked against Julio's legs, and they piled more driftwood and brush over him until he could barely see out.

Julio squirmed against the rope. The stiff jute cut into his skin; his hands were getting numb. At least, Zar hadn't blindfolded him.

Julio pressed his eyes closed. Tensing, mustering all his strength, he kicked out with twisted, doubled legs. The bones of his upper arms wrenched in his shoulder sockets, sending a lightning jolt of pain through his body. The prickly heap of brush shifted, jabbed his face, stabbed his neck and chest, but that was all. The ropes held tight.

He leaned his head back against the tree trunk, fighting the pain. Rain streamed from his hair, through his eyebrows, into his eyes, over his nose, and oozed into the gag, diluting the taste of blood. The gag pressed down on his tongue, forcing his lower jaw back and open and cutting into his windpipe so he could barely swallow. "Uuuuuuhhh! Uuuuuuhhh!" Julio's voice strained through the gag. "Uuuuuuhhh!"

If he heard, Zar paid no attention, and neither did Gallatin.

The flooding stream was rising. Rushing water had reached his moccasins and was creeping up his legs.

By twisting his head, Julio could see through a slit between the branches and twigs.

Rain poured in a stream from Zar's hat brim as he slipped the last bar of gold bullion into his saddlebag. "Sure that's all of 'em?"

Gallatin thrust the shovel into the crumbling mud bank at the edge of the water. "We never reckoned on the water risin' this high," Gallatin answered, his voice stretched tight. "But we gotta get goin', Zar, even if we missed some. Them Pawnee—"

Another thunder shock ripped the sky. The rain surged.

"Uuuuhhh!" Julio tried to call out. The creek was undercutting the mud beneath him. Would they stand by and let him drown? The storm was getting worse, not easing off. The edge of the stream lapped at his waist. How much faster, how much higher could this small stream rise?

With lightning and thunder smacking overhead, the sheep would scatter even farther. He had to get away from Zar and Gallatin. Had to get loose, had to get back. One dog, one man—Chivita and Dick—couldn't handle all those sheep without him.

Keep thinking of me, Grandfather. Don't give up. I can't die here! I won't! Teresita, Silent Walker, Santa María. *Ayúdenme!* Help me.

Zar swung into his saddle. "Ride back and get the rest of our gear and some food from the sheep wagon. If that slave sees you, tell him—tell him we was gatherin' up strays when the storm hit hard. Tell him we seen Julio fixin' to head 'em away from the creek and that little Injun pony threw him. Hit his head on the rocks down below. Flood washed his body away 'fore we could get to him. Tell him that. Bent, too, if you happen onto him. Tell them I'm lookin' for Julio's body."

"Zar, I cain't tell a story like that very convincin'. 'Sides, they'd come over here, lookin'," Gallatin whined. "We both gotta go back. "

"With saddlebags bulgin' with gold? Back in Missouri, we got a $500 reward on each of our heads. It don't make no sense carryin' evidence so's everybody'd see it, now does it, li'l brother?"

"Then you ride Heck. Leave Jesse here with me. You've got all the gold on Jesse." Gallatin sneaked a look toward his brother. "You wouldn't go off without me, would ya, Zar? Take all the gold?"

Yes, he would! Julio thought, twisting his arms, searching again for some slack in the ropes.

"Well, I ain't goin' and leavin' you here with him." Zar squinted toward where Julio was buried beneath the brush. "You're so sweethearted, you're liable to cut that Messican-lovin' sheepherder loose. Then we'd be marking notches in a prison wall, sure."

Julio squirmed. "Gallatin!" he tried to yell.

"We gotta stick together, Zar. Then if Pawnees come back, we can fight 'em off together."

"Pawnees ain't gonna' be pickin' no fight in rain like this. Go on! I'll wait here."

"We gotta have our bedrolls, Zar. It's still gonna be days 'fore we're back home." Gallatin's voice was quivering. "But if we want our gear, we both gotta go. I ain't goin' without you."

"Gallatin Searcy, you little—" Zar spurred his horse and bore down on Gallatin, one arm raised ready to strike.

Gallatin flinched, but he stood his ground. He shouldered the rifle, and said, "Both of us go, Zar. Or neither one."

Zar's face. From what Julio could glimpse between leaves, he had never seen such fury contained in a human face. Gallatin, he thought, now that you've finally stood up to Zar, you'll never be safe from him again, even if he is your brother. He'll kill you as easy as he killed Chivita's puppy. As easy as he's tryin' to kill me. You'd better know that.

Zar jerked viciously at Jesse's reins, cutting her mouth with the bit. "Let's go then."

Julio heard Jesse's hoofs slap the water as Zar galloped away. Gallatin thrust his rifle into its scabbard, but before he could mount, Zar thundered back in the opposite direction along the edge of the roiling water.

"Pawnee!" Zar yelled. "They're comin'! Ride, Gallatin, ride!"

Julio peered through the opening in the leaves. Jesse galloped past, hoofs throwing chunks of mud, splaying muddy water through the brush pile and into his face. Zar leaned forward in the saddle, kicking with both heels and beating Jesse with his hat while the heavy saddlebags pounded her sides.

Gallatin leaped into his saddle. He charged past Julio, swinging the rifle. Heck's hoofs struck inches from Julio's doubled knees. Julio shrank back and turned his head, protecting his eyes. Gallatin's rifle swept down. Branches cracked, shifted, scattered. The hiding place was destroyed.

Julio opened his eyes, blinking away mud, and realized what had happened. Thank you, Gallatin, he thought. At least, now there's a chance someone might see me.

Gallatin's horse had already overtaken Zar's heavily loaded mule. Riding bareback, three braves were in close pursuit. Three others, looking surprised, slowed in midstream, staring down at Julio. One had an injured left arm.

The wounded brave's pony was unpainted, or if it had been painted, the rain had washed away most of the design. The round shield hanging at the pony's side was decorated with symbols and fringed with scalps. The brave whooped victoriously, raised his lance, and pointed it directly at Julio's heart.

In the distance, thunder rumbled. Julio shook his head, flipping rain from his eyes and nose. "Uuuuuuhhh!" He tried to speak through the gag, but could not, and with his hands bound he could not sign. The brave's intent was clear. He would count coup—touch him, wound him, kill him. Tied and gagged, Julio was still fair game, as much as a Cheyenne brave staked to the ground at the line of battle.

It is my time to die. Spring was Dancing Feather's time to die. Summer is mine, Julio thought. The yellow bear claw pressed into his chest under the loops of rope. The Pawnee will finish your job now, grizzly. And with that thought, a wave of calm passed over him. This is my time. My time to die. I'm sorry, Grandfather, but it's all right. Nothing lives long. . . . My time, Papá, but it's all right. I'll be with you. Somewhere deep inside a chant began, calling forth the Cheyenne name Dancing Feather had bestowed upon him.

> I am Soaring Eagle
> I rise high
> To Great Spirit
> I rise high
> I am Soaring Eagle
> I rise high
> To Great Spirit, I rise

The scent of crushed sage surrounded him. The rhythm of remembered drums encompassed him. The chant lifted his spirit from his bound body. He could see everything now, everyone, himself, half submerged, tied to a flooded tree. Mamá. Teresita. Little Gabriela. Silent Walker. They passed before him, smiling, as if in a dream. Chivita! Ay! Chivita! Take good care of her for me, Dick. Papá!

> Soaring Eagle, I rise high
> Nothing lives long

Lance poised, the brave advanced, but he seemed lost in time, each of his pony's strides slower, slower. The spray of muddy water lifting, lifting, lifting from its hoofs.

Suddenly the pony shied and danced sideways, throwing its head. Its nostrils flared.

Julio jolted back inside his body. A quick warmth flowed through him, and he recognized the presence of the great power he had felt on the Purgatory. Is it you, Dancing Feather, one last time?

The Pawnee ponies pranced, nickered, jerked at their bridles, their eyes wild. Twisting, clinging to his pony's mane, the wounded brave stared openmouthed. The lance froze in his grip; his attack halted.

The three braves stared up, up, up—six, eight, ten, twelve feet into the air—terrified, transfixed. They could not look away. They could not move.

Julio could not see a thing. But for a second, he caught a lingering scent of crushed sage and the echo of the haunting word he had heard on the Purgatory: "Protector."

19

As suddenly as the ponies had spooked, they began to calm. The braves looked from right to left, bewildered. For several moments, none of them spoke. Then in a language Julio had never heard all three burst into speech, gesturing, their voices filled with awe.

Julio shivered in the swirling water. What had the Pawnee braves seen?

The man Zar had shot focused intently on Julio. His eyes were not hostile now. They were filled with surprise—and something else. Was it respect? Fear?

Julio blinked away rain, for the first time really seeing the brave's features. He was tall, proud, with a cleft beneath his lip in the middle of his chin. The top half-inch of the upper edges of his ears had been trimmed so they draped down over the middle of his ear like a cord. Both earlobes had also been cut and hung in elaborate carved loops with openings as big as a brave's thumb.

Julio's pulse throbbed in his wrenched shoulders. His breath hissed around the edges of the gag. Mucus ran from his nose. Wounded Brave, cut me loose!

Glancing nervously from side to side and up into the air, the wounded brave drew his knife and crept toward Julio. Leaning forward yet staying as far away as possible, he sliced through the rope once near the knot. "Ho!" he exclaimed, edging back as the coils fell away from the bear-claw necklace. His eyes stretched wide and even wider when he saw the scars on Julio's arm. *"Kuruks!"* he exclaimed. He motioned to the other two braves, who inched forward to see.

With the rope loosened, Julio's chest heaved. He could move again, but his teeth were chattering uncontrollably. He was shivering in spasms.

The wounded brave quickly sliced through the last loops that tied Julio's ankles and wrists, then backed away.

Slowly, painfully Julio stretched his numb limbs and stiff joints. A moan seeped through the gag. Blood swooshed through the veins in his arms like rushing sparks of fire. When he could move his fingers again, he tugged the gag from his mouth. He thrust his jaw out and upward. The jaw hinges popped, and finally he could close his mouth. "Thank you," he tried to say to Wounded Brave, but his voice croaked like a bullfrog. Gratefully he lifted his trembling hand to make the sign of peace.

Cautiously Wounded Brave reached out and pulled Julio to his feet in the swirling water.

Mud oozed down Julio's pants and inside his moccasins as he stumbled from the stream and up the slippery bank, grabbing bushes for support. He staggered upright when he reached a level ledge just as the other braves returned, whooping and waving in the pouring rain. Their ponies picked their way, one after another, through the trees and brush on the opposite side of Owl Creek. The last Pawnee was leading Zar's mule, Jesse, and carrying a long pole with a bloody glob of wet, dirty gray hair dangling from the tip.

Julio's stomach lurched. He looked away, but he couldn't escape the truth of what he saw or the image that rose in his memory—Papá by the stream. He swallowed hard, tasting bile. At least, it was only one scalp, not two. He hoped Gallatin and Heck had gotten away.

With a triumphant shout, Wounded Brave galloped forward to accept the trophy. He shook it high in the air; then gesturing wildly he told the returning braves what had happened. He nodded toward Julio and to the tree where Julio had been tied. Then he raised his good arm—up, up, up—and tensed his hand into a claw.

Another brave leaped forward, hunching his shoulders, walking stiff-legged, swaying from side to side. His fingers curved and spread wide. His lips pulled back. His nose wrinkled. Repeatedly his mouth opened; he gnashed out with his teeth and roared.

The returning braves watched wide-eyed. *"Kuruks!"* they exclaimed. Wounded Brave reached for Jesse and pointed at Julio, and the other braves nodded agreement.

Wounded Brave tugged Jesse toward Julio, but she shied, slamming Wounded Brave broadside with her saddle. Wounded Brave flinched and grabbed his arm. Frowning, he felt the outside of Zar's saddlebag and the bulging hard-edged objects inside that had bumped against him. Trying to lift the saddlebag, he exclaimed aloud to his companions, then untied the straps, reached in, and pulled out a bar of gold. Turning the shrunken leather covering over and over in his hands, he tested its weight. He smelled it. Saying something to the other braves, he passed it around. Then one bar after another they emptied both saddlebags into the stream.

"You. Come," Wounded Brave said, holding out Jesse's reins to Julio.

Julio's breath caught in his throat. Wounded Brave speaks English! He'll understand! "I'm a sheepherder for William Bent," Julio said. "Many sheep. I have to get back to the flock." His voice was still raspy, shaky. "Back to the wagon train. To Independence." He pointed in the direction of the trail.

"You. Come," Wounded Brave repeated, motioning for Julio to mount Jesse.

"No! I have to take care of the sheep. And my dog and her puppies! I have to go to my grandfather. I have to go!" Julio pointed again, making his voice strong. Without waiting for another response, heart galloping, Julio turned his back to the braves and thrust his moccasins into the mud, digging toeholds into the embankment.

"*Teradeda!*" Wounded Brave said. He said other words too, but Julio heard that one sound over and over again.

"*Teradeda! Teradeda!*" The other braves joined in the warning.

Julio glanced over his shoulder, but they had not drawn their bows or lances.

Wounded Brave's pony circled in front of Julio, blocking the way. "You come!" Wounded Brave insisted, sliding from his pony and slapping Jesse's saddle. "*Teradeda.*" He nodded toward the trail and spoke again in his own language, talking for a long time with great emotion. He was explaining something important, it seemed, but the only words Julio recognized were *teradeda* and *kuruks*. *Kuruks* must mean bear. He didn't know what the other word meant, but several times when Wounded

Brave said, *teradeda*, he scowled at his grizzled trophy on the end of the stick.

Just before he reached his foot into Jesse's stirrup, Julio knelt quickly, scooped up a bar of gold bullion from the mud, and slipped it into Jesse's saddlebag. It might help him somehow, somewhere. Julio slid his leg over Jesse, stretching to straddle her wide, flat back. She was almost twice the size of Pinta and these braves' ponies. Would she be as fast? Could she get him away from the Pawnee? Julio looked up toward the edge of the ravine with one last hope of seeing Dick or Chivita.

Wounded Brave motioned Julio to ride behind him, in front of the others. "You. Come."

"You. Come," were to be the only English words Julio would hear for many days.

20

Tun-tun, tun-tun, tun-tun. Like distant drums, the ponies'
hoofs beat a steady rhythm through meadows so high that
sometimes Julio had to stand in Jesse's stirrups to see
over the drooping heads of the grasses.

All Julio could think about was how cold he was from
the floodwater, but as the rain slackened and Jesse kept
pace with Wounded Brave, he began to warm up. His
shaking subsided, and he was lulled by the animal's gentle
gait, though he missed Pinta and the soft sheepskin saddle.
Jesse's back was much wider, and the stiff leather saddle
was hard as stone.

Tun-tun, tun-tun, tun-tun. Zar and Gallatin had left
him to die. If it hadn't been for the grizzly spirit or Dancing
Feather or whatever it was, Wounded Brave would have
killed him. That glob on the end of the stick would have
been yellow not gray. But I'm still alive. As he warmed,
that simple realization filled him with a peaceful dreamlike
joy. I'm still alive! I will see Silent Walker again. And
Teresita and my other sisters! And Néške'e and Mamá!
And I will find my grandfather in Independence.

Tun-tun, tun-tun, tun-tun. They were all with me.
They are all with me now—Papá, Dancing Feather, Silent
Walker, Teresita, Mamá, my grizzly. . . . Tun-tun, tun-
tun, tun-tun.

The braves followed a narrow trail that wove in and out of groves of thick trees, trees unlike any in Taos or along the Arkansas River. Trees with three-pointed leaves, trees with narrow leaves, trees with shiny drooping leaves, all of them beautiful shades of green. Shafts of light angled through the branches, and Jesse's big hoofs stepped softly on wet green grass. Everything here was green.

A bird Julio had never heard before warbled overhead reminding him of Teresita. Teresita loved the songs of the birds so much that Uncle Rumaldo called her his meadowlark. *Teresita, you would love this birdsong.*

Tun-tun, tun-tun, tun-tun. He envisioned Teresita in their small single-room house with Mamá and all his sisters. He saw Mamá's handwoven rug spread carefully in the center of the dirt floor. He saw the corner where Mamá hung her herbs and the beds rolled up along the walls. He imagined little Gabriela lifting the edges of her skirt, dancing. He smelled beans simmering and heard the chickens—and Mamá scolding—and a longing almost like pain passed through him.

Tun! Ta-ta tun-tun! Tun-tun, tun, tun. One of the ponies stumbled, snorted, then the peaceful pace resumed.

Teresita would love these trees, the thick green grass. So would Silent Walker. He sighed. *Silent Walker.* Thinking of her felt like warm sunshine. Dreamily Julio focused down on his left foot and on the silhouette of the grizzly-eagle Silent Walker had beaded onto his moccasins. *How strange that she had seen the grizzly attack him in her dream. And she was waiting for me when I returned. I hope she didn't see Wounded Brave charge me with that lance. I hope she sees that I'm all right now.*

It didn't seem strange that Teresita knew these kinds of things. They had been together since they were babies. He and Silent Walker had only known each other since early spring, yet Silent Walker shared his vision too. She saw the grizzly spirit. In some mysterious way, they were linked. Even with the scars, her face was soft and shy and made him want to reach out to touch her dark eyes and her shining hair. He wished she were with him now to see the sun hanging below the clouds in the west, shooting crimson rays through the leaves.

West!

Julio jolted to his senses. He stared at the sunset. If that's west, then I'm heading northeast! Ay, Dios!

I am not all right! I'm a Pawnee captive. And these braves are taking me northeast—in the wrong direction!

Chivita! The puppies! Dick! William Bent! They must think I'm dead! How will they get the sheep across the Little Arkansas without my help? If Bent took the wagons through Owl Creek before the downpour, who was left to drive the sheep wagon? Dick can't do everything!

"Wounded Brave!" Julio called out, not knowing what else to call him. "I must go back!"

Wounded Brave turned and looked at him, but his pony didn't slow, and he didn't reply.

"If you don't speak English, do you speak Spanish? *Habla usted español?*"

Wounded Brave did not respond.

"French? *Parlez-vous français?*"

Still, no response.

"I have to go back!" Julio pulled the reins across Jesse's neck, turning her. But the braves behind him grinned and blocked his way.

Wounded Brave watched, looking amused, as the braves' small ponies herded Jesse back into line.

The Pawnee no longer seemed a threat, yet no matter what Julio said or how many times he gestured and tried to turn back, they would not let him go. Why did they want him? Where were they taking him? If only I could talk with them, he thought. If only I could make them understand why I have to get to Independence, they would help me the way the Cheyenne did.

They rode that night by moonlight through wispy clouds, all that remained of the storm, stopping when the moon set. Julio ate the pemmican and jerky the braves gave him, drank from a tiny brook, and huddled on a bed of fresh-cut leaves, determined not to fall asleep.

When he heard the gentle breathing of the six braves, he sat up as noiselessly as he could. Arms and shoulders aching from Zar's binding, he stood slowly, carefully. He hoped Jesse wouldn't bray and the Pawnee ponies wouldn't nicker and give him away. He would take only the saddle blanket, the saddlebags, a fast Pawnee pony and leave Jesse and her big, heavy saddle behind.

He had taken only a few steps when a hand closed firmly around his ankle. A voice in the dark said something softly. It didn't sound angry.

"I have to make water," Julio whispered, gesturing in a way any man would understand, and soon returned to his bed of leaves.

He wouldn't sleep; he'd try again later. His fingers crept into the leather bag at his waist. At least he had his things—his flute, Teresita's white stone, his knife, his flints, some bits of sage, and his slingshot. Enough. He could survive. He might not find the wagon train, but if he headed south and east, he would either cross the Santa Fe Trail or come to the big river, the Missouri. Either way he was sure to find Kansas Landing or Independence— eventually.

Independence. I will find you, Grandfather. He imagined the old man, tall and straight with silver hair, waiting, listening the way Silent Walker and Teresita did, for his thoughts. I'll find you somehow. I'll show you where our names are written together in the family Bible—

Julio's heart slammed inside his chest.

The Bible! I don't have it! I don't have it anymore! It's in the sheep wagon. Ay, Dios! Without the Bible, how can I show who I am?

21

Julio tried to escape two more times that first night. The next night Wounded Brave took Julio's leather bag away and tied Julio's left wrist to his own right wrist on the sides opposite their injuries. *"Kuruks,"* Wounded Brave said, pointing to Julio's bear-claw wound. He touched the wound on his own arm, then pointed again, this time to Zar's scalp. *"Teradeda."* He said something more in a solemn tone, then lay back and closed his eyes. Julio had no choice but to lie down too. When either one moved, both would be awake. Wounded Brave would feel every breath he breathed. Julio could not sneak away.

The farther north he rode, the longer they were apart, the more Julio missed Chivita. Being without her was like being without part of himself. He missed Dick and worried about him and the sheep. He wondered about Gallatin. He glanced at the trophy on Wounded Brave's shield and tried not to think of Zar. Most of all, he missed his freedom. He had to get on to Independence and his grandfather.

On the morning following the third night that Julio slept bound wrist-to-wrist with Wounded Brave, he sensed a change. The braves bathed in the stream. Their talk was lively, and as they glanced his way, he heard again and again the word, *kuruks*, and when they said that word, the braves looked at him with wonder. Wounded Brave nudged Julio toward the stream, gesturing that he, too, should bathe. He did. Laughing, the other braves tried to braid his wet hair, but he shook his head, and they let him go.

They broke camp early and urged their ponies on faster than before. Julio felt the excitement rising. Something was about to happen.

The terrain sloped downward. Julio guessed they were coming to a river valley, maybe to a Pawnee village. The first signs of people were fields—small fields of corn planted in straight lines, hills of squash and pumpkins, melons, bunches of sunflowers, and rows of ripening tomatoes. Some vegetable patches were surrounded by pole fences. These are like the fields around Taos, Julio thought. Are the braves taking me to an American settlement? Could this be Independence?

Twenty or thirty footpaths angled from the fields and surrounding woods, merging onto the main path. Now Julio saw people working the fields. Not white people, but dark-skinned women, using tools much like the ones back home. One woman was clearing weeds with a long-handled hoe made from the sharpened shoulder blade of a buffalo. Another woman was using a rake made of deer antlers. The rake, too, had a long pole handle. Other women were harvesting corn, beans, onions. Good tools. Good crops. And good horses. A large fenced corral surrounded horses of every kind, stout, tall horses Americans rode, ponies from the plains, even a few Mexican burros, and one lone mule.

Julio stared at the bright red tomatoes and shiny squash with longing. His stomach rumbled and his mouth watered. Ahead he saw coming into view the rounded tops of *hornos*. So the Pawnee bake in adobe ovens here, just the way we do in Taos! The memory of the sweet, rich smell of biscochuelos swept over him. Biscochuelos, the way Tia Inez made them, biscochuelos sprinkled with sugar, the way Teresita and Mamá made them. "Jesse, do they bake biscochuelos here?" He leaned forward in the saddle, sniffing the air.

But as he rode closer, he saw the mud domes were not ovens at all. They were houses, mound houses with tunnel-like vestibules leading inside. Each house was much larger than Mamá's adobe casita. The village was a maze of closely set mound houses, with pathways winding every-which-way among them. The pathways were cluttered with horses and children and chickens and piglets. This settlement was much more like a Mexican town than any Cheyenne village, except that there were no goats or sheep, and no black-and-white sheep dogs like Chivita.

Julio and the braves followed Wounded Brave single file through the winding streets into the village. Thin sliced meat was hanging to dry on racks along the narrow passages. Ears of red-and-purple corn braided together by the husks also hung to dry. Several old women were lounging on the roofs, weaving onions together by their tops. The women waved, calling out greetings. Younger men and women rushed up onto the dome-shaped roofs shouting and waving.

Good smells of charcoal smoke and cooking mixed with the smells of people and animals living in a close space, but the rich scent of parching corn overwhelmed the sour and made Julio want to leap from Jesse's back and ask for food. In Silent Walker's village he would have, but here, although the people were watching him and talking about him, no one had greeted him yet. He still didn't know why he was here. Was he a captive, a guest, a slave? Soon he would know. But he was more curious than afraid, for the braves had treated him well.

Earlobes swaying, Wounded Brave led his procession into a large cleared area in the center of the lodges, like the plaza where people gathered in Taos. Proudly he raised his trophy pole, and the people cheered. Then he leaped down from his pony and opened one of the panniers, reached inside the square leather box, and grabbed a handful of coarse gray salt. Slowly he let the salt trickle through his fingers back into the box. Again the people cheered.

Salt! Finally Julio knew. These braves had been on an expedition to harvest salt. That was why they approached the wagon train. They'd wanted to trade salt for coffee or sugar or beads. And for this, Zar had shot at them!

Wounded Brave led his pony to the front of a lodge whose entrance faced onto the clearing. This lodge was twice as big as the others. Julio imagined it was a chief's house or a grand ceremonial lodge where the tribe gathered.

"You. Come." Wounded Brave motioned Julio to dismount, and once again the people cheered.

Julio swung down from Jesse's back. "Whoa, Jesse. It's been a long ride. I don't know what will happen now. I may never see you again, but these are good people." He stroked her neck. "They'll treat you better than Zar did." He tried not to glance at Wounded Brave's pole.

Jesse curled her neck toward him and nuzzled his hand as if she understood. Julio uncinched the saddle and swung the saddle and the saddlebags onto the ground next to the great lodge. He spread the saddle blanket over the saddle to dry, then ran his hand over Jesse's sweaty back, wishing for a brush.

Wounded Brave left his pony beside Jesse, but he did not lead Julio into the big lodge. He took him into another of the lodges that faced the center, next to the largest one. Long white lodge poles leaned on the outside wall—lodge poles. So, Julio thought, the Pawnee use tipis too. They must take their tipis to the plains to hunt buffalo. Julio ducked his head as he went through the vestibule and blinked through the smoky haze inside. Wounded Brave guided him to a place near the center of the mound house and pushed down on his shoulder. Julio sat, feeling a smooth woven mat beneath him. Behind him he heard Wounded Brave leave.

At first, Julio could see little more than flames in the fire pit and shafts of light filtering down through the center hole in the roof. Then little by little his eyes adjusted, and he looked around the lodge at tools, saddles, robes, and a tripod holding what looked like a painted shield. Beds covered by mats of woven rushes set on short legs along the curved wall. A curtain of rushes hung over sections of the room. Many families must share this lodge, Julio thought, but each family can close the curtain to be alone.

A woman wrapped in a smoothly scraped suede dress approached Julio, head lowered, arms extended. She knelt silently and handed him a buffalo-horn spoon and a wooden bowl of steaming food—squash and some kind of white root cooked in a broth of chunky meat—then left as quietly as she had appeared. When he finished eating, the woman appeared again, head lowered, arms extended, carrying fresh tomatoes and corn and squash.

"Thank you," Julio said. *"Merci."*

She retreated in silence.

Even though his hunger had been satisfied, he bit into one of the ripe tomatoes, savoring its tart juices, biting down on slick yellow seeds that popped between his teeth. When Wounded Brave returned, Julio offered him a tomato, but the warrior refused, motioning Julio to come with him.

Now, Julio thought, I will meet the chief and learn why Wounded Brave has brought me here. Then I will go on my way.

Blinking in the bright sunlight, Julio followed Wounded Brave, carrying the vegetables. But again he was not taken to the grand lodge, rather into a second lodge on the opposite side. He was seated and served another feast which, except for the roasted corn, he could barely eat. When he finished, the second woman presented him with gifts of wampum—strings of purple and white shells and beads—and left him alone.

The Pawnee are treating me like a chief from another tribe, he thought. Is it because of the spirit of the grizzly— or whatever the braves saw at Owl Creek? I don't know, but if they think I am special, they'll surely let me leave. If they think of me as a chief, I should act that way. Julio considered the three most important people he'd known— William Bent, Father Martinez, White Buffalo. I must speak as they do, with power and honor, not as a prisoner or slave.

He hoped, once Wounded Brave took him to his chief and told his story, Wounded Brave would guide him to Independence himself. He had come to like Wounded Brave and respect his gentle patient ways.

After Julio's third feast in a third lodge, instead of saying thank you for the gifts, he motioned to the vegetables and wampum on the woven pumpkin-skin mat beside him. He stood, walked outside, nodded toward the saddle, and the woman put the gifts in the saddlebags.

Julio stood alone outside in the courtyard. Evening was falling. Light was fading across the roofs of the mound houses, leaving the tunnel-like alleyways below in darkness. Men came and went from the grand lodge. Inside Julio caught a glimpse of the flames from a large fire and heard drumming and a phrase, "High-e-ye-ye," chanted over and over again. People were hurrying here and there, watching him with curiosity.

Were they preparing for a ceremony like a Cheyenne sweat lodge? Would they burn sweet grass? There was no sage here. He hadn't seen sage growing since he left the Arkansas. He fingered the dried sage in his leather bag and lifted his fingers to his nose to breathe in the haunting scent. Would these people honor the same Great Spirit as the Cheyenne? How different from Taos, Father Martinez, and the Catholic Dios. What would Grandfather believe? Would he understand the saints or the sacred sage, or do Americans believe another way like Mr. Bent? He imagined that one day, when his grandfather asked about everything that had happened to him, this night with the Pawnee would be another story to tell.

The first stars had begun to appear when Wounded Brave returned. He was dressed in what must have been his most elaborate clothing—a high fur cap topped with two eagle feathers, a fringed, beaded leather shirt, and black-and-white striped leggings. The holes in his ears were decorated, top and bottom, with seashells and bright red-and-yellow tassels. He was riding a fresh, eager-eyed pony and leading another, and a boy about nine years old walked beside him. The boy's hair was cropped short; he seemed stiff, uncomfortable.

"Hello," the boy said, glancing up at Julio. Then quickly he looked away.

"You speak English!"

"Yes," the boy replied, eyes downcast. "My American name is Thomas. I learn English in the missionary school. I will trade talk for you."

Julio understood the word *school*. Later he would ask about *missionary*. With a translator, he could make Wounded Brave understand that he must get to Independence. "I'm Julio," he said.

"The braves call you White Grizzly." Thomas sneaked a look into Julio's eyes. "They say you have great power."

"White Grizzly?"

"They say the spirit of the white grizzly protects you," Thomas said.

Julio thought of the name Dancing Feather had given him, Soaring Eagle. He had earned that name, but not White Grizzly. White Grizzly—the name pulled him back to the Purgatory . . . the old grizzly with broken teeth . . . the grizzly spirit that embraced him . . . the grizzly spirit at Owl Creek . . . Whatever that power was, it had come to him. He had no power of his own.

"What is he called?" Julio looked at Wounded Brave, but spoke to Thomas.

"Coming-Around-With-The-Wind does not have an American name. He is the son of Chief Seven Bears. He wants me to say his father asks to trade this pony for your mule. He says this mule is too fine to ride as a pony. It

should be ridden only in high ceremonies. We have two"—
he seemed to be hunting for the right word— "leaders in
this village. Only one mule. Now we have a mule for each."

Julio was surprised. Jesse was his only because
Wounded Brave—Coming-Around-With-The-Wind—said
so. The Pawnee could simply have taken her. Julio signed
yes to Wounded Brave and reached for the pony.

Wounded Brave nodded. The seashells and yellow
tassles bobbed in his ears.

A name. A pony. Julio was honored. He imagined
riding up to the door of Grandfather's store in the company
of Pawnee dressed in their finest clothing. With these
braves, he realized, I may have already traveled faster—
much faster—and farther than if I'd been driving sheep.
With them, I may even get to my grandfather sooner.

He looked at the faces that had gathered around him.
Like the Cheyenne, these were good people, well groomed
and well dressed, except one woman whose clothing was
as tattered and dirty as her unkempt hair. She shuffled
by, head downcast.

Julio saw Wounded Brave watching him. Wounded
Brave spoke, and Thomas translated, "She is a mother
who mourns. Her son, Lone Tree, was killed in the spring
during a battle on the Kits ka, the Longest River Running
East, the river the Americans call the Arkansas."

Wounded Brave spoke again, gesturing toward the
great lodge.

Thomas translated. "Coming-Around-With-The-Wind
says he will now present you to his father, our chief, and
to our old"—Thomas paused as if he were searching for a
word Julio could understand—"priest."

22

Two men sat in positions of importance in the center of the great lodge near the fire, facing the door. Julio focused immediately on the one with expectant eyes. An enormous collar of bear claws fanned across his chest—not one claw as in the necklace Julio wore, but thirty or forty white claws gleaming like a smile. Draped over the man's shoulders was a grizzly hide with hand-sized five-pointed stars decorating the side opposite the fur.

"It is for this I am called Seven Bears," the chief spoke, fingering the collar. "My name has changed with each bear I have killed." He gestured for Julio to sit in the place of honor, facing him. "Sit, White Grizzly. For many seasons, we have been expecting you."

"This is our chief," Thomas whispered the translation. "He is called Seven Bears. He says, 'For many seasons, we have been expecting you.'"

For many seasons? Expecting me? Julio did not know what he meant.

Remembering how important gift giving was with the Cheyenne, how he'd given Silent Walker his only possession, Papá's coffeepot, Julio said, "Seven Bears, may I present you with a gift?" Julio leaned toward Thomas. "Thomas, will you bring in the saddle I left outside?"

Seven Bears nodded and smiled as Thomas dropped the heavy saddle before him. But noticing the unsmiling face of the priest, Julio wished he had another gift to give as well.

"I see," Seven Bears said, reaching out toward Julio's arm and necklace, "you too have met the grizzly." Back and forth, Thomas translated. "You are on a journey."

"Yes."

"You go in search of your people."

"Yes."

"You are American, but you do not know American ways. Is this true?"

"Yes." On the journey from Owl Creek, Wounded Brave had not understood anything he had said. How could Seven Bears know this? Who could have told him? "I lived with my family far away in Mexico," Julio explained. "Now I go to Independence to find my American family."

As Thomas translated, Seven Bears' eyebrows knotted more and more closely together.

"Independence, the white man's settlement. It lies downstream on the *Kis paruks ti*, the Beautiful River," Thomas translated, "the Missouri. It used to be the land of many tribes. You will not like it there."

Then am I free to go? Julio asked silently.

"White men, the men of Independence, are not Spirit Callers. They are not Seers of Spirits. They are not as we are. You are not as they are. They will not understand you."

Seven Bears cast a long, sideways glance at the priest. They conversed in low voices, which grew into fierce grumbling, back and forth, back and forth. Thomas did not translate.

"I say it is him!" Seven Bears said loudly, and these words Thomas did repeat.

"Coming-Around-With-The-Wind"—the priest gestured impatiently to Wounded Brave—"tell us what you saw!"

With great solemnity, Wounded Brave rose and told his story of harvesting salt, riding toward the wagons to trade salt for lambs, being shot, taking revenge on the two white men. He thrust the shield bearing Zar's scalp into the air, and the braves around the walls of the lodge yelped their approval.

Then Wounded Brave motioned for the other two braves who had been at Owl Creek to join him. Together they reenacted the rest of the story: Julio tied to the tree in the rising stream; Wounded Brave charging, aiming his spear; the grizzly spirit roaring up before him, snarling, clawing, blocking the attack, rearing taller and taller, protecting Julio; Wounded Brave shrinking back. Suddenly the grizzly-brave somersaulted into the crowd and was gone.

Julio watched Seven Bears' eyes flame, and he saw the stoniness of the priest's face too. The priest rose to his feet, arms raised. "This boy cannot be a Spirit Caller." His voice sounded like the caw of a crow. "He is not from a priestly line. He has not been trained. He is a white man. White men do not call spirits. White men know nothing of calling spirits."

Thomas's voice whispered quickly into Julio's ear, rushing to keep up. The crowd calmed.

"He is a white man," Seven Bears agreed, "but he does not know the ways of the white man. From long ago, I remember the vision of Owl-Watching-Below: A white man will appear among the tribes, a white man carrying the mark of a bear, a white man who is not like a white man, a white man who is just, a white man who speaks straight, a white man who will teach other white men the world of spirit." Seven Bears' voice was firm as stone. "This young man is protected by the Grizzly Spirit. He has powerful medicine. He is the one." Seven Bears looked directly at Julio. "You are the one."

Julio understood even before Thomas repeated the last words, "You are the one."

Slowly the priest stood pulling his lank old body erect, his neck long and hard. He stared at Julio through snakelike eyes. "If you are a Spirit Caller," he said, "call the White Grizzly. Now!"

Thomas gasped. Coming-Around-With-The-Wind and his two companions stared, white-eyed, and shrank toward the wall of the lodge.

Seven Bears frowned, then slowly nodded to Julio.

"Call the White Grizzly," Thomas repeated.

Smoke stung Julio's eyes.

"They want you to show them what the braves saw." Thomas's voice trembled. "The priest wants to see the Grizzly Spirit."

Julio sensed the growing tension in the room, and as Thomas translated he turned toward him so he could look around. The only way out was the main entrance through the vestibule behind him.

"The white boy is no caller of spirits!" The priest's voice rose triumphantly. "What is your name?" the priest demanded.

"Tell him your name!" Thomas hissed.

Julio sucked in a deep breath of smoky air. Speak with power, he reminded himself. I'm not a captive. Not a slave. "In Mexico," he replied in a strong voice, "Julio Montoya. The Cheyenne call me Soaring Eagle. In the United States, my name will be William Allen Forester." When Thomas translated, a low rumble of voices rose among the braves.

The rumble crescendoed, but the cry of one brave rose above all the rest. *"Teradeda!"* That was the word Julio heard at Owl Creek. The word Wounded Brave had said over and over again, shaking Zar's dirty gray scalp.

"Teradeda! He is the friend of our enemy, the Cheyenne!" the brave shouted. Like a hornet, Thomas buzzed in Julio's ear. "He says you were there on the Kits ka where Lone Tree was killed. You were there with the Cheyenne!" Arms raised, the brave leaped over the seated men toward Julio.

Julio sprang to his feet, and his hand crept toward his knife. That brave! He had seen him before. Other braves held Julio's attacker, but as he strained forward yelling, *"Teradeda,"* Julio saw the purple zigzag scar over his eye, and he knew. This was the brave who had rushed toward him on the smoky bank of the Arkansas. This was the brave who had counted coup.

Chief Seven Bears' voice was no longer friendly. "Is this true? You fought with the Cheyenne on the Kits ka?"

"No," Julio spoke loudly. "Thomas, tell him I did not fight in the battle. I'd been attacked by this grizzly." He ran his fingers over the raised white scars on his arm. "I was lying in a wagon, wounded. I saw this brave, and he saw me." Julio turned directly toward his accuser. "You saw me. Was I fighting? Thomas, ask him. Was I fighting?"

Thomas's translation faltered. "He says, 'Not fighting. You were with the Cheyenne. You are *teradeda*, friend of the enemy.'"

"Call the Grizzly Spirit!" the priest's shrill voice spiraled over the shouts of the braves. "Let the Grizzly Spirit save you from the enemy now!"

Thomas scrambled away, but Julio didn't need an interpreter to understand. The braves were choosing between the priest and the chief. Their voices thundered; they gestured wildly. Suddenly the lodge erupted into swirling motion, and braves converged on him from every direction but one. On the opposite side of the fire pit, Seven Bears flung open his great grizzly robe and rushed across the center of the lodge, closing that one last route to escape.

The fire flickered. The flames dipped low and disappeared into the logs, leaving only red glowing coals. Then from that glow a sudden burst of white smoke filled the dome of the lodge with the unmistakable figure of a growling white grizzly. Teeth bared, claws raised, eyes dark voids in the smoke, the grizzly shape hovered above them.

The braves shrank back, hands flung high. This time Julio saw the phantom, and he, too, edged away. Sweat beaded on his face, and a chill scraped his bones. In the trembling silence, he stared up at the towering ghost.

Suddenly, without warning, the great weight of Seven Bears' robe landed on Julio's shoulders. He cried out as his knees buckled and he sank onto the dirt floor. Cowering, he peered up at the grizzly claws gleaming across Seven Bears' chest. Seven Bears raised both arms and nodded sharply to Thomas.

Seven Bears' eyes bored into the priest's eyes, and in a commanding voice he spoke. "He is the one!" Thomas whispered, keeping as far away from Julio as he could. "This boy has called the Grizzly Spirit."

The priest, brittle as a strip of old jerky, narrowed his eyes. His breath rasped in and out, in and out, but finally he gestured for the braves to sit, and as they did the fire flared to life, dissipating the last wisp of the apparition. Seven Bears lifted the grizzly robe from Julio's shoulders and gestured toward the door.

Weak-kneed, Julio rose, turned, and followed Seven Bears into the vestibule. His ears told him that Thomas and Wounded Brave followed close behind.

Seven Bears spoke, and Thomas's voice quivered the translation. "Seven Bears says you must go fast. The priest will not agree for long. He will—" Before Thomas could say any more, the priest's stringy voice spiraled behind them to a growing roar of response. "The priest says the Grizzly Spirit was Seven Bears' trick."

Fists clenched, Seven Bears shouted into the lodge.

"It was no trick, Seven Bears says." Thomas paused, listening to Seven Bears. "Now he says you must escape. Go!" Thomas shouted. "We will hold them back as long as we can." Julio and Wounded Brave pivoted and ran from the vestibule entryway. They darted away from the lodge, but Julio tripped and sprawled facedown in the dirt. The lodge poles! He'd tripped over the lodge poles. The lodge poles—their way to escape. "Ay, gracias!" Julio cried. He scrambled up, wildly pushing and kicking and shoving the long smooth poles toward the entry door. Laughing, Wounded Brave leaped aside as one after another the poles rolled down the rounded roof, raking against dried mud, bumping and bouncing against each other, clattering into a logjam behind them.

Julio grabbed the saddlebags and the lead rope of one of the ponies. Wounded Brave took the other pony. "Adios, Jesse." Julio pulled the pony into a dark passageway and threw the saddlebags over her. Behind them he heard the startled cries and groans of their pursuers as feet and shins tangled with lodge poles.

Julio raced ahead, Wounded Brave right behind him, but the passageways circled around and around. The village was a death trap. Nothing was straight. Leaning forward, he rode past mound houses that all looked alike, but found himself heading back toward the angry voices. Wounded Brave shouted and pointed to another narrow alley. Chickens squawked and scurried from under their ponies' feet while pigs squealed and fled out of their way. Julio could hear hoofbeats of other ponies in pursuit.

Twisting and turning, they dashed past the glow of fires flickering inside lodges, past dark passageways and tunnel-like streets, dead ends.

Julio gripped the pony's mane, kicking her to go faster, faster, on toward the friendly fields of corn, past the pumpkins, past the squash, farther and farther away from the cries in the village.

23

Julio jarred awake. His heart crashed in his ears. "Chivita! What is it?" He staggered to his feet, struggling to breathe the humid morning air. He was clutching his flute. He didn't remember taking it out; he didn't remember stopping to sleep. But now he did remember—Chivita wasn't with him anymore.

Whish-whop! Whish-whop! Whish-whop! A rhythmic chopping sound pulsed through the thick woods.

He thrust the flute into his bag and grabbed his slingshot and stones, ready, wary. Ignoring the itching insect bites that covered his body and the sweat that coated his skin, he peered into the wall of vegetation.

Then the same loud moan that had jarred him awake jolted him again. The moan lifted and wailed above the churning whish-whop, whish-whop louder and longer than the cry of any owl, louder and longer than the breath of any living being he had ever heard. The hair on the back of his neck prickled.

Julio crouched, waiting, but the leaves and grass didn't stir. Whatever was making the sound was not close. Not Pawnee, not the friends of the priest. His breath rushed out, but when he tried to breathe deeply, he couldn't. His chest was heavy. The air was heavy. He felt as if he were suffocating.

Whish-whop! Whish-whop! Whish-whop! Whish-whop!

What is it? The mysterious sound was coming from farther away than he'd first thought and seemed to be moving. He crept forward, then stopped, remembering the Pawnee ponies and the saddlebags. And Wounded Brave. Had Wounded Brave turned back without telling him?

He glanced around, then exclaimed aloud, "Ay, Dios!" The saddlebags lay in a heap on the ground. I must have gone to sleep, slid off, and pulled them with me, Julio thought.

He and Wounded Brave had ridden all night through thick woods. When they could no longer hear the other ponies behind them, they'd stopped in a clearing to find their bearings from a star in the north that never moved. But now, in daylight, with the sun hidden in haze and no star to guide him, every direction looked the same. No mountains loomed up as markers. One hill looked the same as the next, covered with trees and vines and undergrowth so thick he couldn't see. Without Wounded Brave, he would not know which way to go.

He shouldered the saddlebags and followed the pony's tracks only a few yards before he found not one pony, but four. Sleeping beside the ponies lay Wounded Brave and, with him, Seven Bears and Thomas. Seven Bears did not have his heavy grizzly-skin robe any longer, but he still wore the necklace of claws.

"Gracias a Dios!" Julio exclaimed. "You're here! You escaped!"

"White Grizzly!" Thomas jumped to his feet, wide awake. His eyes quickly scanned the trees. "Don't call the Grizzly Spirit again!" he said. "We came to help you!"

"Thomas, I have no power to call spirits."

"But in the lodge, I saw . . . "

Whish-whop! Whish-whop! Whish-whop!

Seven Bears quickly rose to his feet, pointing toward the sound and speaking in a serious tone. Thomas translated.

"Seven Bears says we will guide you to the river. Then we must return to our village before the priest destroys everything."

Julio slid the saddle blanket from his shoulder and spread it over the pony Thomas brought him, balanced the saddlebags across its back, and mounted.

Whish-whop! Whish-whop! Whish-whop!

"What *is* that?" Julio gestured toward the sound, which grew louder and louder as they rode.

"Kis paruks ti. Hurry! You'll see."

The four ponies fought their way through vines and bushes and under the boughs of shaggy trees, downslope toward the sound.

Julio's first glimpse, through branches, was of something bright red and dazzling white, gliding like a giant swooping bird. Then he saw the river—wide, wider than anything he could have imagined, wider by far than the Arkansas—stretching and winding, brown and thick with mud, between high banks of green, edged with sandbars and dotted with ragged islands. The thwocking and hooting and loud moans weren't from a bird or an animal at all. They came from a huge canoe, a painted boat two stories high, with a wheel on the side that turned around and around and around, and a chimney that burped great puffs of black smoke.

"Kis paruks ti! This has to be the Missouri River!" Julio exclaimed. "Ay, Papá, I made it! I'm here! Grandfather, I'll find you soon! Thank you, Seven Bears!"

"Seven Bears says get on the boat. Independence is that way. Good-bye."

"Adios!" Julio grabbed the saddlebags. "Thank you!" He scrambled down the slope through the undergrowth, tripping, falling, startling a doe. He tumbled to a stop at an outcropping of light tan rocks above the river and called out at the top of his voice to the people on board. "Hola! Hello! Will you take me to Independence?"

Whish-whop! Whish-whop! Whish-whop! The wheel continued to churn. Several hands waved, but the huge boat didn't slow. The churning didn't stop. Whish-whop! Whish-whop! Whish-whop!

"Will you take me to Independence?" Julio shouted, but the steady rhythm of the wheel did not falter.

For a long time, Julio stared after the backside of the churning paddle wheel, his dismay overpowered by wonder over this American invention.

Back in the Pawnee village, Seven Bears had said, "You will not like it there."

Back at Bent's Fort, William Bent had said, "You don't know anything about that life. You're too wild, too free. They'd accept you about as soon as they'd accept a Cheyenne. Or a rattlesnake."

Julio scrambled back up the steep slope, through the tangling vines, to the place where he had left Seven Bears, but his Pawnee friends and the four ponies had gone.

Encircled in swarms of tiny biting flies, Julio returned to the edge of the high bank above the Missouri. At least, he was headed in the right direction. If he walked long enough, he would certainly reach Independence.

Sweat ran from his face and under his arms, and the air pressed against his chest and lungs as if it were trying to smother him. On and on he tromped, all day long, until he fell exhausted onto a bed of cool leaves beside the river. Early the next morning he was struggling through the undergrowth along a low bank when he heard a voice floating along the deep swishing water. Someone singing.

> *Sur le pont d'Avignon,*
> *L'on y danse,*
> *L'on y danse,*
> *Sur le pont d'Avignon,*
> *L'on y danse tout en rond.*

Julio grabbed a branch and leaned out over the murky river. Another boat floated lazily around a bend near the shore, a squat, square box with low sides, carrying barrels standing on end around the edges and more barrels roped together in the middle of the deck. A tall, skinny man, loose-jointed as a wooden puppet, balanced at the back gently pushing and pulling a single long oar, guiding the boat away from snags, and singing, Julio thought, like an angel sent from heaven.

> *Les beaux messieurs font comm' ça*
> *Et puis encor' comm' ça.*
> *Sur le pont d'Avignon,*
> *L'on y danse,*
> *L'on y danse. . . .*

"Hello, Monsieur, hello! Hello!" Julio waved. "Hello, over here!"

Abruptly the singing broke off, and the boatman looked his way. "Allo!"

"Is this the Missouri River, Monsieur?"

"Oui!" The boatman flipped the flat cloth hat from his head and bowed. "Le Beeg Muddy."

"Independence?" Julio shouted, pointing downstream.

"Oui!" the boatman answered with a sweep of his arm.

"Will you take me?"

"Of course, mon ami"— the boatman shrugged— "but I cannot stop. You can swim?"

"No!" Without a second thought, Julio heaved the saddlebags onto the deck and jumped into the brown, swirling water.

"The oar, mon ami!" the boatman cried. "Grab the oar!"

24

The boatman sang and talked a mix of French and English.

"Bent's Fort," Julio answered, shaking water from his ears. He thought the boatman had asked where he came from. "Before that, Taos."

"Far away!" The boatman pointed from the raised white scars on Julio's arm to his bear claw necklace.

"Yes, grizzly."

"*Sacre bleu!*" He nodded, then smiling, shook Julio's hand. "*Je m'appelle François.*" His long bony fingers felt like wooden sticks in Julio's palm.

"I'm Julio."

The boatman suddenly looked into the water at the side of the flatboat. "Grand dieu!" He pulled hard at the oar, yelling at Julio for help. Julio grabbed the oar and felt the great force of the river tugging at the smooth wood beneath his hands. François stabbed a second side oar into the water and pushed away from the snarling limbs of the dead tree surfacing from the depths.

"*La rivière est dangereuse,*" François said, as the boat rounded a bend, now a safe distance from the tree.

When François wasn't talking, he was singing. Soon his voice and the current slurping against the low sides of the flatboat lulled Julio into a deep sleep. It was dark when he awakened. His stomach twisted and grumbled, and his mouth watered at the wonderful smell of fried fish.

François had pulled ashore and was singing over a small fire and dancing—it seemed—with his frying pan. Julio stood and stretched.

"Hongry, Julio?" François waved. "Come. *Mange*, eat."

They feasted on fish from the river and Pawnee corn from Julio's saddlebag that Julio roasted on the coals. François talked and François sang, and after a few sips from his jug, Julio joined in an action song that mimicked fancy ladies and musicians, and seamstresses, and marching soldiers crossing the bridge d'Avignon. Laughing and swatting at mosquitoes, they tottered back on board.

"Bonne nuit, mon ami," François sang, draping his arm over Julio's shoulders.

"Bonne nuit, François." The boat rocked, and Julio's head felt as if it might swirl up from the back of his neck. "Sweet dreams," he said, sinking onto the deck.

In the morning, François looked like a dog after a dog fight. His hair stuck out in every direction, and his feet weren't dancing. "Who es thees Silent Walker? *Une fille, n'est-ce pas?* A girl? You talk to her all night long, mon ami. And Chivita? Who es she? *Beaucoup de femmes*! Many women, mon ami! And you are so young."

"I-I'm sorry." Julio ears flamed, and he changed the topic quickly. "When will we get to Independence?"

"Eef we have no problem," François said, floating his arms in the air, "by afternoon tomorrow."

"Tomorrow? We're almost there?"

"Tomorrow, Independence!" François howled up at the sky. "Tomorrow, women, Julio! Women and wine and song!"

Julio didn't howl; he didn't shout. His search was almost over. Now he would finally know.

He turned away from François and, balancing carefully, walked as far to the front of the boat as he could. He straddled a wooden barrel and gazed out over the coffee-colored water, water the color of Néške?e's brown soup. If my grandfather's still there, still alive. . . . What if my grandfather is gone?

"Independence." Without asking, Julio knew they had to be near. His stomach knotted. He squinted toward the place where boats gathered along the bank.

"Oui!" François laughed, crossing himself. His feet danced a little jig. "*Nous sommes arrivés.* We're here!" He pointed up from the river, past the large paddleboat that had docked and was being unloaded, and past another even larger boat with an even larger paddle not on the side, but in back. Whistles and horns tooted from the two boats, and the sound mixed with the music of banjos and floated toward them across the water.

Julio followed François's pointing finger up to the top of a steep bluff of sand-colored stones that looked like an enormous stack of dried adobe bricks. "I don't see a town," he said.

"Non, mon ami. You cannot see her. Les Américains, they build their town of Franklin on the reever, and she washes away." François grinned over a gaping hole where a front tooth had been. "Maintenant, les Américains, they build Independence high up on top, and she never washes away. She is up there, hidden in trees." He scratched under his small, flat hat.

"You perhaps go to—how does one say? —courthouse in Independence? The building with the tall tower?" He shoved his hand up in the air as high as it would reach.

"No." It wasn't just the humid air and muggy heat that made it hard to breathe now. A spurt of excitement radiated from Julio's chest, quickly replaced with another rush like the one he'd felt when the grizzly loomed up in the grass before him. "I'm looking for my grandfather."

"*Ton grand-père! Formidable!* I know many people here. *Comment s'appelle-t-il, ton grand-pére?*"

"His name? Myron Forester."

"Oui! Oui!" the Frenchman exclaimed, his feet dancing below the long oar. "*Un homme très bon,* a good man, mon ami! I knew him. Every time in Independence, I trade in his store. I am sorry he go."

"Go?"

"*Oui, il est parti.*" The man slipped his flat cloth hat from his head. His feet stood still.

"My grandfather has gone?"

On the landing, Julio waved good-bye to François, then plodded numbly away from the river, past canoes, tipis, rough wooden shelters, and through the bustle of wagons and donkey carts, mules, oxen, and horses. People of every sort and every color passed by him, joking and laughing and talking a jumble of languages.

Not knowing what else to do, he started up the white stony road to the town with the weight of the saddlebags pulling on his shoulder. Maybe someone there could tell him when and where his grandfather had gone. But another journey, another thousand miles? Or two? Or three? Would he go on? Could he? Would those invisible ropes that tugged from the west stretch that much farther east? And without the Bible. . . .

A cart loaded with barrels and boxes from the big boat rumbled up beside him, the wheels slipping and crunching on stone. "Hop on." The driver nodded to the wagon bed. "It's a fur piece to walk."

Julio heard the little boy riding beside the man ask, "Is that a white-haired Injun, Poppi?"

"Cain't reckon *what* he is, son," the driver said. "I've seen Scots and Irish and Frenchmen and Mexicans on this landing. And I've seen Chinamen and English and Germans and Kentuckians and Texans. I've seen trappers and traders that are more Injun than Injuns, and I've seen Pawnee and Kansa and Osage and Potawatomi and Cheyenne"— he flicked his whip beside the mules' ears— "but, son, I ain't never seen nobody with the looks a' that one before."

The way the wagon driver talked was the way Zar and Gallatin talked. Gallatin. Was he alive? If he escaped, where had he gone? Back to help Dick? Back to Owl Creek to dig for overlooked gold? Back to Texas?

Julio settled himself on the bed of the bouncy wagon, feet dangling, and approached Independence facing backward, staring down on the wide muddy river the Pawnee called "Beautiful."

Sweat wept from his skin. He was wet and clammy all over, so hot his head ached and throbbed. The air was heavy and smelled of the river bottom, of muck and fish and a recently threatened skunk.

Welts from insect bites covered his chest under Dancing Feather's bear-claw necklace. Three parallel white scars rose from his arm. He studied his clothes. The

American-made trousers from Bent's Fort were wet and
frayed and shiny with grease. The beads on his moccasins
were coated with mud. The leather bag at his side had
worn thin. Cheyenne moccasins, American trousers, a
Mexican bag. My clothes are like me, he thought, Mexican-
American-Cheyenne. Everything. Nothing.

It was a "fur piece" up the bluff to Independence. After
the first mile winding up the steep bank, Julio realized
the driver hadn't been talking about buffalo robes or beaver
pelts. When he said "fur piece," he meant "far."

The wagon crested the top of the bluff and followed
the rolling wooded hills until, finally, Julio saw roofs. The
roofs were not round like Pawnee lodges or pointed like
Cheyenne tipis or flat like the flat tops of adobe houses in
Taos. The houses of Independence were built of wood with
tops like steep mountain slopes. In the center of everything
a large square building rose above all the others with a
spire as high as the tip of an ancient pine.

Julio slid from the wagon. "Thank you, sir." His
moccasins squished into a street mucky with droppings of
mule, oxen, and horses and muddy from rain. He stared
at the numbers of people and shops. His ears rang with
the din from blacksmiths' sheds where men hammered
wagon wheels and shod horses. As he began to walk, he
caught bits of talk from the people who picked or sloshed
their way through the arrow-straight streets, the way he
and Teresita had snatched new words from the streets of
Taos.

" . . . Northerners got no right to tell us how we should
live. . . ."

"Texas! He went out there?"

" . . . and the children in school . . . "

"I don't know. I don't trust Polk. . . ."

" . . . calico . . . trimmed with white lace . . . "

Three men were engaged in such a heated debate they almost ran into him.

"We'd win!"

"Of course we'd win, George. Mexico wouldn't have a chance. But is it right for the United States to drum up a false reason for war, simply to get more votes for the South?"

"Hogwash!"

"George is right. Do you think votes are what this is about? You're dead wrong if you do! Have you read what this reporter, John O'Sullivan, says? It's right here in the *United States Magazine and Democratic Review*." The man waved a paper in front of the other man's face. "Read this! It'll change your mind, for sure!"

Two men with ruddy skin and wild red hair wearing brightly colored skirts woven in squares of red and green and blue swaggered through the mud. Round knobs bobbled on top of their strange flat caps. Loose-jointed Frenchmen walked and talked like François.

Dark-skinned women wearing leather and light-skinned women wearing calico passed each other without speaking, but one young woman in leather made his heart leap. For a second, he thought she was Silent Walker.

Men and women as dark as Dick and Charlotte Green pulled carts and carried heavy loads and laughed. Were they slaves too? Tall bronzed men who walked like kings wore elaborate clothing of bright-colored felt and high top hats with feather plumes. Their language sounded different from anything Julio had ever heard. So many people, so many languages, but no one spoke to him. A bare-chested old man dressed in leather sat cross-legged against a wall. He looked as bewildered as Julio felt by the sight of so many white people.

The high haze was lifting now, and a white-gauzy sun strained to shine on the tall spire of the tallest house, the one François had called "courthouse." That must be like Father Martinez's church in Taos, Julio thought, where people pray or like the lodge of the Cheyenne where wise men talk. It may be the lodge where my grandfather sat. Later I'll go there and ask where he has gone, but first I want to see where he has been.

He gestured to a rider on a horse with a well-brushed tail. "Mr. Myron Forester's store? Can you tell me where it was?"

"Right over there, lad." The rider pointed to a boxy building with a wooden boardwalk in front.

Julio walked slowly toward the store, his moccasins heavy with mud. The store was dark inside, and the door was closed. No one was coming or going.

The gold lettering was still on the window just as Charlotte had described it. Julio reached up and touched the swirls of gold and black that made the words *Myron Forester*. Inside the window, the displays were gone, and through the window Julio could see empty counters. Only a few burlap sacks slumped here and there on the floor. An empty scale hung from the ceiling.

He pushed against the door, then remembering the latched door of the trade room at Bent's Fort, pressed down on the curved metal thumb piece. The latch clicked, and with a creak the door swung open.

"Hello?" Julio stepped inside onto a floor so polished it looked as if he were walking on water. He could still smell the lingering scent of the merchandise—tobacco, coffee, rope.

"Hello? Is anybody here?" He peered through the dim light. The store was empty, but he could feel his grandfather's presence. It was a fine store, clean and peaceful. Here his grandfather had treated people well, honestly, and with respect.

From behind a curtained door in the back came a rustle, and a wafting scent of tobacco tickled his nose.

"Frank? Is that you?" a deep bass voice called out, and a tall, slender gentleman with silver hair stepped from behind the curtain. He wore a dark suit and a white shirt with a high collar. A black rope looped around the collar and tied in front. In one hand, he carried a large satchel, in the other, a pipe.

"Well, hello, young man! You're not Frank. Good morning," he said in a kind voice. "May I help you?" He gestured with the pipe toward the empty shelves, and with a faint smile said, "I'm afraid there's nothing left to sell you, though. The store is closed."

Julio's heart swelled in his chest. *It's him! I know it's him!* "M-Mr. Forester?"

"Yes." The gentleman nodded and set his satchel on the floor.

"You are Mr. Myron Forester?"

"Yes. I am." Mr. Forester stepped forward, looking more closely into Julio's face, frowning slightly at his grimy pants and feet.

"Mr. Forester . . . I'm Julio Montoya. No, I-I mean, I'm—" Julio let out the pent-up air that threatened to explode inside. "Mr. Forester, you've been searching for the family of your son, yes? He—they took a wagon westward a long time ago, maybe ten years?" My words are coming out all wrong! Julio thought. His knees began to tremble. "Mr. Forester, I had a Bible with our names to show you who I am, but I don't have it anymore. It's still in the sheep wagon."

Mr. Forester's pipe suddenly froze in midair. Slowly, without looking away from Julio's eyes, he circled until Julio faced the light from the window. "John!" His voice was barely audible. He lifted the long straw locks of hair from Julio's forehead. "You look just like my son John."

Julio waited for a long silent moment before he said, "I'm sorry. I don't remember him, but the writing in the Bible says that I am his son. It says he was my father . . . and my real name is William. William Forester. William Allen Forester." He swallowed hard. "Mr. Forester, that means I-I am your grandson."

Time stopped.

Julio gazed into his grandfather's green-brown eyes. Neither Julio nor his grandfather blinked, neither looked away, neither smiled or laughed or spoke.

"I thought you would never come," the old man whispered.

"I thought you had gone," Julio's voice choked in his throat.

"Almost." The pipe lowered. "Oh, Billy, my boy," he said, "I have waited so long." He held out his hand.

Julio's hand slid into his grandfather's, and that small touch carried him forward. His arms wrapped themselves around his grandfather and his face pressed hard against the smooth white shirt. Tears burned the backs of his eyelids.

"Oh!" Grandfather exclaimed. "Oh!" His arms hung as stiffly as two branches from a tree, but Julio could hear his grandfather's heart race. Then slowly, Grandfather's arms encircled him, holding him gently as if he were afraid Julio would break. As if he had not hugged another person for many years.

Awkwardly, hesitantly, he stepped away. He slipped his glasses from the bridge of his nose. Blinking rapidly, he wiped the lenses with a white handkerchief from his pocket. "Mmm," he said. "Hum. Yes." He slipped the glasses back into place. "It has been such a long, long time. . . ." He breathed deeply—once, twice, three times. Then he asked, "Your father and mother? Your sister?"

When Julio didn't answer, a wave of sadness passed over his grandfather's face. Slowly, a silver tear slid through the smile-wrinkles on his cheeks. He walked to the window, hands grasped stiffly behind his back, and looked outside. *How many times has he stood there, watching for us that way?* Julio wondered. Then he heard a deep intake of breath and his grandfather turned to face him again. "They are gone. Now I know. But you are alive, and you have come. Finally, Billy, you have come."

25

Sometimes Julio didn't understand Grandfather's fancy words and long sentences. Sometimes Grandfather didn't understand Julio, but Julio's spirit soared. As they sat on empty crates facing each other in the empty room, love and laughter laced their bungling conversation with understanding. With his grandfather he felt different from the way he had felt with anyone else as far back as he could remember.

"Did your Mexican family treat you well, Billy?"

"Papá and Mamá? I am their son." Julio shrugged. "But I look different. My friends call me Green Eyes." Julio laughed lightly. "I have eight sisters. Eight, Grandfather! Teresita, Eugenia, María, Consuelo, Constancia"—for a second, he was home with them again—"Gabriela . . . "

"Stop, stop!" Chuckling, Grandfather raised his pipe. "I'll never remember so many new names!" He shook his head. Julio's grandfather was slow to speak, but silence stretched comfortably between his words. His gaze lingered on the bear claw against Julio's chest. "You are much like your father. So much like him." He sighed. "But you have grown up in another world. What has happened to you there?"

Someday, Julio thought, I will tell him everything. I'll tell him about the grizzly out on the Purgatory and the grizzly spirit that protected me at Owl Creek and in the Pawnee lodge. I'll tell him the prophecy of Seven Bears. But he remembered Seven Bears' warning, "They will not understand you." Briefly Julio told only what happened at Owl Creek.

"But the Smith brothers' name wasn't Smith," Julio said, pulling the saddlebags to his side. "You know them. Their name is Searcy. They were two of the bandits who robbed Don Antonio, the two who escaped."

Grandfather's pipe paused midair. "Well, I'll be! Christopher and Gallatin Searcy! So they've finally come to light, have they?"

"They were in Texas before they joined the wagon train from Bent's Fort. They ran off at Owl Creek. I found them digging up bars of gold like this." Julio reached down through what was left of the Pawnee corn and smashed tomatoes to the bottom. He felt, then felt again, then emptied everything onto the floor. The leather-covered gold bullion was not there. In its place was an ordinary chunk of white crumbly rock. Had the Pawnee woman taken the gold? No! Immediately he knew what had happened—the night on the boat, the singing, the jug, François. He stuffed the corn and squash back inside the saddlebags. "Well, Grandfather, I did have one of Don Antonio's bars of gold."

"Stolen?"

"Yes, stolen and stolen and stolen again."

"Never mind." Grandfather reached over and gently touched the scar on Julio's arm. "We have something far more lasting than gold. We have two lifetimes of stories to tell each other," he said, "and we have each other. Do you remember anything—from before? From when you were little?" He reached inside his suit coat and drew out a small hard-covered packet tied with ribbon. "This is your family," he said softly, opening the cover and touching the small painting. "You. Your father, John. This is your mother, Anna, with your sister, Sarah, in her arms."

"My mother?" Julio's breath caught in his throat. "Then I do remember her! It's—she's the—Santa María, the—" Hand trembling, Julio held the picture close. He struggled to find the words in English. The woman in the picture was the dream woman with yellow hair he'd seen in his visions. "For a long time, I thought she was an angel."

"An angel," Grandfather repeated softly.

"She came. I saw her the night Papá died. She sang— she sang— this." In a wobbly voice, Julio pieced together the remembered words.

> How can there be a cherry
> Without no stone?
> How can there be a chicken
> Without no bone?
> How can there be a ring
> Without no end?
> How can there be a baby
> With no cryin'?

Julio's grandfather slipped the corner of his white handkerchief under his eyeglasses, then cleared his throat. "Your mother sang that song over and over again when you were little. You loved it so. Do you remember the other verse that answers the questions?" In his a deep bass voice, he began,

> A cherry when it's bloomin'
> It has no stone.
> A chicken when it's pippin'
> It has no bone.
> A ring when it's rollin'
> It has no end.

One voice high, one voice low, Julio and his grandfather sang the final words together.

> A baby when its sleeping
> Has no cryin'.

"No cryin'!" Grandfather laughed, dabbing his eyes, and once again they were in each others' arms, and this time Grandfather's embrace was not stiff.

"Billy, you have family in Pennsylvania—aunts and uncles and cousins on both your father's and your mother's sides of the family." He eased back down onto the crate. "Oh, and your Grandmother Martha! She will be overjoyed to know you are alive."

"A grandmother? I have a grandmother?"

"Yes." His grandfather's smile became sad, wistful. "Your Grandmother Forester passed away . . . not long after you disappeared. But your mother's mother is alive, and the last I heard still well."

"Can she read? Would you write a message to her for me?"

Hurried footsteps sounded on the boardwalk outside. Someone knocked, and the door burst open. "Myron, are you ready?"

"Frank!" he exclaimed. "This is Billy! Billy's here!"

A broad-shouldered young man was outlined against the light from the open door. "Who?"

Grandfather pushed himself up from the crate, stepped forward, and rested his hand lightly on Julio's bare shoulder. "Frank, this is John's son . . . my grandson . . . William, Julio . . . Oh, my! What shall I call you?"

So much is in a name, Julio thought. William, Julio, Soaring Eagle, White Grizzly. "Grandfather," he said slowly, "I'd like you to call me what you have called me ever since I was born."

"Then I will call you Billy." He smiled. "Will you call me Granddad?"

"Granddad." Julio felt a grin stretch across his face. "I like that, Granddad."

"Billy Forester, this is my friend, Frank Henry."

Julio stood. "Mucho gusto." The words accidentally slipped out in Spanish, and Julio quickly switched languages. "I'm glad to meet you."

Frank's large hand pumped up and down, up and down. "He speaks English, Myron."

"Yes. Quite well, considering."

"You're the answer to prayers." Frank finally stopped pumping and released his grip. His bushy eyebrows rippled as he frowned into Julio's face. "Under the grime, you even look a bit like your granddad." He winked. "How did you ever find your way back here, Billy?"

Billy. How strange it feels to be called by that name, Julio thought. Before he could attempt to answer, a long whistle floated up from the river, and Frank reached for Grandfather's satchel. "Is this what's left?"

"Yes." Grandfather nodded. "Julio, where are your things?"

Julio lifted Zar's saddlebags and shrugged the shoulder where his leather bag hung. "This is all I have."

"Then we'd better be on our way." Frank stepped outside.

A growing wariness crept through Julio's body, a feeling like the warnings that came to him in the meadow at night when something was stalking the sheep. "Go where?" he asked.

"Home." Granddad's voice caressed the word with softness. "Home."

Not until Frank Henry's horse-drawn wagon rolled past the last houses of Independence and started down the steep road to the dock did Julio ask, "Granddad"—he turned to watch the expression on his face—"where is home?"

"Why, Pennsylvania, of course." Then his granddad's eyes opened wide in surprise. "Oh, I'm sorry, Billy. You don't know! You can't possibly know. My household goods are loaded on the sternwheeler bound for Saint Louis. From Saint Louis, we'll travel overland to Pennsylvania. You came just in time. One day later and we would not have found each other." He shook his head. "It's a miracle that we did."

26

The sternwheeler loomed before them, balanced on the dark water, one row of windows stacked on another, in lines as straight as the streets of Independence. The paddle on the back was not turning yet, but smoke belched from the smokestacks into the dim afternoon sky. Julio could feel the riverboat huffing like an anxious ox ready to move.

"It's all right, Billy." His grandfather paused at the top of the wooden gangplank and called back. "We'll buy your ticket on board."

But at the base of the ramp, Julio stepped aside. A boarding passenger, a man wearing a tall beaver hat, edged toward the far rail of the gangplank as if he were afraid Julio would soil his clothes. Men with straining muscles carried huge stacks of firewood from the dock and up a different loading ramp. I should be with them, Julio thought, looking down at his bare chest.

"Billy, please come." Trembling, his granddad's outstretched hand lifted and came to rest on his chest over his heart.

How can I leave without Chivita? Without knowing what has happened to Dick and Mr. Bent and the sheep? How much farther will this boat take me from Silent Walker and Néške°e, and Mamá and my sisters?

Those invisible ropes stretched, stretched now so hard, so tight, they threatened to rip him apart. But as he looked at the old man who had waited for so long, he stepped onto the ramp and crossed to the boat, his moccasins thudding on the wood like the hollow beat of a drum.

Soon paddles churned, water surged, and the sternwheeler pulsed steadily downstream. On deck, Julio's granddad slept sitting straight upright, the cold pipe resting on his leg, spilling tobacco.

At the railing, Julio stood alone. Between his thumb and forefinger, he rubbed Dancing Feather's grizzly claw back and forth, back and forth, in time with the paddle.

A blue heron swooped up from the green shadows along the western bank of the river, its neck doubled into an S as it glided over the water. Julio judged the distance to shore. Kansas Landing was on that side; Bent's farm was there somewhere. Whish-whop! Whish-whop!

The paddleboat's steady rhythm echoed Julio's turmoil, sweeping him back into memories, back in time.

Whish-whop
Back to the Purgatory, the grizzly attack
Whish-whop
The Grizzly Spirit rising up, Protector!
Whish-whop
Whish-whop
Whish-whop
Silent Walker, Silent Walker, Silent Walker.

Over and over the swishing water sang her name.

Whish-whop
Whish-whop
Seven Bears' prophecy.
"This young man is protected by the Grizzly Spirit.
He has powerful medicine.
He is the one."

Words, images, faces, rose like submerged logs.

"You are a fine young warrior, Soaring Eagle.
Follow your path.
You will return to the land of the grizzly."
Whish-whop
Whish-whop
"You are a peacemaker like your papá.
The West needs men like you."
Whish-whop
Whish-whop
"You are the one. You are the one.
You are the one."
Whish-whop
"You have grown up in a different world."
Whish-whop
Whish-whop

Slowly, like settling water, his mind began to clear.
"Yes, a different world." Julio knelt on the deck and reached
into his leather bag for his flute. Quietly, he slid onto the
bench beside his sleeping granddad. With barely any
breath, he played the notes that had comforted him at every
turn on the trail. Granddad would need that comfort now.

As the final tone of Julio's song drifted away, Granddad shifted in his seat. "I must have fallen asleep. That was beautiful, Billy."

"Granddad"—Julio took in a deep breath—"I can't go to Pennsylvania with you. I can't leave without Chivita, and I have to know what happened to Dick Green and Mr. Bent's sheep."

Granddad's head bowed so low Julio could not see his eyes. Then he looked up, smiling slightly. "Of course, you must stay. You belong in the West, and I"—he straightened on the bench—"I will go home."

"Granddad, would you stay with me this winter at Kansas Landing? Chivita and I could work at Bent's Farm. We could take care of the sheep that survived. In the evenings, you could tell me the stories of our family." Warmth rushed to Julio's face as the words tumbled out. "Teach me American ways, and how to read and write. Tell me what Americans believe about Dios and Great Spirit. Teach me everything you know!"

Granddad rose slowly from the bench, crossed to the rail, and leaned into the breeze. Julio could not see his face, but he could sense the battle raging inside.

"Granddad, you must know war is coming between the United States and Mexico. They're both my countries. The Cheyenne are my people too. And so are you! I have to learn before I can choose where to go and what to do."

"Billy," his granddad said, turning slowly, "the first moment I saw you, I saw your father. In the second moment, I saw a savage and feared there was no hope. Now I see a young man already rich in wisdom."

27

Julio sheered the thick wool from the hind legs of the last old ewe. "Qué calor! It's too hot for wearing all this wool, no, Señora Oveja?" he said. He raised a fistful of wool high into the air, then dropped it onto the pile.

"Finished!" Dick tossed his clippers onto the wool. "Mah poor back!" Slowly he straightened. "I shouldn't ought to say this, Mr. Julio-Billy, but right now I ain't sorry we lost all them sheep at Owl Creek."

Julio laughed. "Me neither!" Dick had called him by both names so many times in the past two weeks that now Mr. Julio-Billy sounded like just one word. Julio signaled to Chivita. *Take them back.* Chivita sprang into action, ears flying, a black-and-white puppy chasing at her heels. Crossing to the water trough, Julio plunged his head into the cool water. He scrubbed with the store-bought soap William Bent had given them and quickly rinsed all over.

Bent had gone to trade pelts in Independence. When he returned, the wagons that had carried buffalo robes would be loaded with supplies and merchandise for trade, and a new wagon train would head west. "Dick, will Charlotte let you keep the puppy?"

"No question 'bout it!" Dick laughed. "Ol' Charlotte, she talks mean sometimes, but she ain't mah boss. No way I ain't gonna keep this puppy."

This close to the Missouri River Bent's Farm was even hotter and muggier than it had been in Independence. William Bent promised that the fall would be beautiful, though, with the bright colors of the changing hardwood trees, and the winter would be cold. Colder than Bent's Fort or Taos. But the growing piles of firewood from the surrounding woods and the stone fireplace that covered one wall of the log cabin would keep him and his granddad warm. There would not be too much work, only tending the animals and taking care of themselves and the farm. A whole winter to study, a whole winter to learn, a whole winter to prepare for what was to come.

Julio tossed the towel beside the trough. "We're finished, Granddad. Can—may," remembering the rule, he corrected himself, "may I study now, while there's still daylight?"

"Of course!" Granddad's face broke into a wide smile as he set aside the book he was reading. He was wearing a loose cotton shirt, open at the neck, and baggy pants. His shoes and stockings were tucked neatly beneath the bench, and his pale white heels rested on the ground. In spite of the hot, muggy heat at Kansas Landing, he looked relaxed, rested. "What would you like?" Granddad asked, lacing his fingers behind his head. "More family stories? Mathematics? Religion? History?"

Julio picked up his slate from the bench beneath a giant oak and sat beside his granddad. "Everything!" he answered. "I want to learn everything you can teach me."

Julio held the chalk and carefully began to write. *E-n-r-i-q-u-e.* "In the spring," he said, "on my way to Taos, I'll carve this name by Papá's grave." Julio set the slate aside. Perhaps it was too soon, but the words ached to be said. "Granddad, will you go with me to Mexico to meet my other family?"

Granddad smiled. He lifted his pipe, struck a match, puffed . . . and puffed . . . shook his head and puffed again. "Autumn hasn't arrived yet. Let's wait and see what spring will bring." He opened the pages of the Bible that had belonged to Julio's parents. "Try to read this," he said, flipping to somewhere in the middle and pointing to a large number three.

Julio held the Bible flat on the palm of one hand, tracking the words with his finger. His reading was still choppy, but if he broke the words apart, he could connect the symbols with sounds he already knew. "For every-thing—everything—there is a sea-son." He held his finger on the word *season*. "I see why you chose this." He continued to read aloud. "A time to be born, and a time to die."

He remembered Dancing Feather's words, "Nothing lives long, only the earth and the mountains."

"A time to kill, and a time to heal; a time to weep, and a time to laugh."

He read the phrase "a time to" over and over again like a simple song, and the lines ran deep and true. The Pawnee priest didn't understand when he said that white men know nothing of calling spirits. From this book, Julio could see that Americans, at least some Americans, knew the world of spirit too. "There are wise people in every nation, aren't there, Granddad?" he said. "Mexican? Cheyenne? Pawnee? American?" Remembering François, he laughed. "Maybe even French."

"Without a doubt." Smiling, Granddad leaned toward the Bible, adjusted his glasses, and read in his deep bass voice.

"A time to mourn, and a time to dance; a time to cast away stones, and a time to gather stones together."

Through the leather bag, Julio fingered the stones for his sling. As long as he was a shepherd, the only stones he would cast would be aimed at coyotes or foxes.

"A time for war, and a time for peace."

Julio let the Bible rest on his knee. "Granddad, I don't know what's going to happen, but there's going to be war between the United States and Mexico," Julio said. "If there is a way I can help this be a time for peace—" Something struck his shoulder, something small and hard.

Heart drumming, Julio leaped to his feet and spun to face the thick woods. He searched right and left and back again, but only a small underripe acorn from the giant oak rolled off the bench beside him. Not a pebble.

Trembling, he thrust the Bible into his Granddad's hands and, dodging through the trees, ran until his side ached and his lungs burned for air. Hands slamming against rough bark to slow his speed, he eased into a lope, then finally to a walk. Last spring seemed so long ago. Next spring so far away. But one small acorn brought both springs together.

He had left Taos with Papá when catkins were budding on the aspen trees last spring, not even half a year ago, not even two seasons. Since then Néške'e, Dancing Feather, Silent Walker, William Bent, Gallatin and Zar, White Grizzly, Wounded Brave, Seven Bears, Granddad.

Julio dropped to his knees in a tiny clearing. The air hung motionless as if holding its breath. Not a single leaf bowed on its stem. Only the throbbing of crickets hummed in the silence. A sudden patter of paws and Chivita and her pup bounded to his side.

He reached into the leather bag that since the very beginning had carried his flute and Teresita's magic white stone. Crushed beneath the crystals for his sisters and the rocks for his sling lay flecks of dry western sage. Lifting a bit of sage, he breathed in the sacred scent, then raised his hand toward the golden swatch of sky above the trees.

"For the springs that have passed and for the springs that will come," he said aloud. "Thank you!" He sprinkled bits of sage toward the north.

"Merci!" Toward the east.

"Gracias!" Toward the south.

The throbbing hum of crickets hushed.

"E-pevaʔe!" Julio flung the last of the sage toward the west onto the deep layer of moldy rotting leaves. He knelt again beside Chivita and her pup and slipped out his bamboo flute. Softly, ever so softly, he blew, and the music of his soul circled out from the banks of the Missouri all the way back to Taos and to his Cheyenne friends and all the way east to Pennsylvania.

Three invisible ropes still held him, three tunes still played, three rhythms beat. But deep within, a new sense of peace settled over the warring tugs, and Julio knew. Finally he knew exactly where he came from, exactly where he belonged.

He knelt and tousled Chivita's ears. "They're all a part of me, Chivita, and I'm a part of all of them. I'm

Mexican *and* Cheyenne *and* American." He grabbed the pup under its round little belly and rubbed his nose against her fur. "I'm like you, Little Pup, a breed of my own."

Author's Notes

Dear Reader,

Thank you for coming along with me on Julio's journey from Bent's Fort to Independence. I hope you enjoyed the trip.

Maybe you write historical fiction or would like to. Maybe you would like to know which parts of this story really happened and which parts I made up. Maybe you find fact more fascinating than fiction.

Many of the characters in the story are based on real people such as William Bent, Dick and Charlotte Green, and Christopher and Gallatin Searcy. The political situation is real as well. In 1845, an oncoming war brewed between the United States and Mexico. Texas, which had been the Independent Republic of Texas, was officially admitted into the Union as the twenty-eighth state. Two years earlier, in 1843, Don Antonio José Chávez had been robbed and murdered in Kansas Territory by fifteen outlaws, including the Searcy brothers. The issue of slavery dividing the United States would lead to Civil War in 1861.

All locations you read about really existed in 1845, and most are still there today—the Santa Fe Trail, Bent's Fort, Big Timbers, Point of Rocks, Pawnee Rock, Owl Creek, Bent's Farm, Kansas Landing (Westport), Independence. In researching for this story, I followed the Santa Fe Trail from Bent's Fort to Independence, found the ravine where Don Antonio José Chávez's body was thrown after he was robbed and murdered, and saw all the places Julio would have seen.

For the purpose of this story, the order of some events has been fictionalized. For example, William Bent traveled the Santa Fe Trail between Bent's Fort and Missouri many times, but he may or may not have led a wagon train in the spring of 1845, the year of this story. We do know that the year before, in the early summer of 1844, floods waterlogged the plains and Bent's wagon train was stranded at Pawnee Fork for a month, then bogged down in mud at Walnut Creek for another month on the journey eastward, all the while, besieged by mosquitoes. By themselves, these facts might be pretty boring, but I think weaving history and fiction together makes facts fun and fiction richer.

—M. P. F.

What's Fact? What's Fiction?

page 1   **Bent's Fort** was built as a trading post in 1833 on the north bank of the Arkansas River, across the river from what was then Mexico and is now Colorado. The Mountain Branch of the Santa Fe Trail passed by Bent's Fort as it crossed the hunting grounds of Native American tribes of the plains halfway between the western border of the United States and Santa Fe, Mexico (now New Mexico). People of many nations came in peace to the Fort to trade—men and women of many tribes and nations, beaver trappers from the United States, buffalo hunters, Mexican merchants, and many others. Bent's Fort was the only building between Independence, Missouri, and Santa Fe, Mexico. For people who had been traveling two months along the Santa Fe Trail, this "Mud Castle" was a welcome site. The Fort was active from 1833 to 1849 when William Bent established a new, smaller fort at the Big Timbers.

page 5 **Cottonwood.** A large broadleaf tree that grows near water in the western United States. Ox yokes, wagons, even wagon wheels were made from cottonwood trees. Support logs called *vigas,* doorframes, and most of the other wood used in building Bent's Fort came from the cottonwoods that grew along the banks of the Arkansas River.

page 6 **Adobe makers.** Skilled adobe makers from Mexico made the adobe bricks and built Bent's Fort.

page 6 **Taos** (pronounced *Tah-os*) was a small settlement in northern Mexico in 1845. Today Taos, New Mexico, has become a center for art and tourism.

page 9 **Father (Padre) Antonio José Martinez,** parish priest of Taos, was a colorful and controversial figure, often at odds with the Bents and other foreigners who conducted business in Mexico and married Mexican women. He brought a printing press to Taos, published a newspaper, and founded a school.

page 10 **Dick and Charlotte Green** were slaves owned by the Bent family. Charlotte called herself the "only lady in de whole damn Indian country." Her taffy pulls and pumpkin pies were favorites with travelers who stopped at Bent's Fort, and she was a favorite dancing partner. Dick was freed after fighting bravely with the Bents in an 1847 uprising in Taos in which William Bent's brother, Charles, was killed. Sometime later, Dick and Charlotte left Bent's Fort.

page 16   **Charlotte's helper.** The white woman cooking with Charlotte could be Mrs. Dale. Mrs. Dale traveled west with her husband and son. Her husband was killed, and Mrs. Dale and seven-year-old Paul were taken captive by Pawnee. Mrs. Dale escaped on a fast Pawnee pony and found her way to Bent's Fort where William Bent gave her work. She stayed hoping that Paul would be found. One day when she was working in the kitchen, a trapper named Blackfoot John walked in and asked for a glass of milk for a boy he had rescued from the Pawnee, taken all the way to Independence, and now had brought back to Bent's Fort. Mrs. Dale screamed. There stood her son, Paul.

page 17   **El Rio de las Animas Perdidas en Purgatorio.** This stream was called "The River of Souls Lost in Purgatory" after early Spanish explorers who died searching for Quivara, Coronado's lost cities of gold. Their bones and armor were found years later. The stream is now commonly called the

"Picketwire." Can you figure out why? Here's a hint: How do you say *purgatory* in French?

page 27 **Sheep.** Records show that coarse-wooled Mexican sheep were brought to Bent's Fort from Mexico and taken on to market in Missouri. Sheep wool *may* have been mixed into adobe as a binder in the bricks Mexican adobe makers made for the construction of Bent's Fort.

page 28 **Kansas Landing**, also known as Westport Landing, became a practical destination for William Bent's eastbound trade. Located on the west side of the Missouri River, Bent's farm raised horses, cattle, buffalo, fodder crops, and provided good grass for trail-weary animals.

page 29 **Don Antonio José Chávez** was a well-known popular trader from a highly respected family of Mexican merchants. In 1843, he was robbed and murdered on the Santa Fe Trail in Kansas Territory by fifteen *banditti*—outlaws— questionably and indirectly commissioned by the Independent Republic of Texas. His body was thrown into Owl Creek. Don Antonio's robbers and murderers were caught, tried, and the two leaders were hanged. Only two men escaped capture: Gallatin and Christopher Searcy disappeared from history into the backwoods of Clay County, Missouri, and were never heard of again. The story of their involvement with William Bent's eastbound wagon train and their return to the site of the crime in 1845 is fictitious.

page 29   **Yoacham's Tavern in Westport** is where the robbers plotted to attack Mexican wagons "for the Texas cause." The plan was commonly known, and enraged citizens petitioned the United States government to stop the bandits. Troops were sent out from Fort Leavenworth too late. Don Antonio Chávez had already been murdered. Before 1843 shipments of gold and silver were safe from bandits on the Santa Fe Trail—so safe that in Independence, fortunes were stacked on wooden boards outside stores, unguarded and unthreatened during the night. Santa Fe Trail commerce was an energetic and exciting link benefiting both the United States and Mexico.

page 29   **Texas.** On March 1, 1845, United States President John Tyler signed a law admitting Texas into the Union. Three days later, the new president, James K. Polk, was sworn into office. News traveled slowly in 1845, and for the purpose of this story, I imagined that Bent learned the "news" on the trail. With the admission of Texas, tensions increased between the United States and Mexico. By June, Polk had sent troops, emigrants, and surveyors to the West, further heightening tensions that culminated in the outbreak of war with Mexico in May 1846.

page 52   **Grizzly attack.** In 1821, a party of American adventurers was attacked by a grizzly in a patch of wild grapes along the Purgatory River. Guns misfired, men ran, and the grizzly caught

Lewis Dawson by the head. Major Jacob Fowler recorded this incident in his journal which was deciphered and published as an important historical document more than seventy years later. His account reads in part, ". . . a gun was fyered off and the Cry of a White Bare Was Raised . . . [the bear] Sprung up and Caught Lewis doson and Pulled Him down In an Instent Conl glanns gun mised fyer or He Wold Have Releved the man. [Dawson] was Son again in the grasp of the Bare . . . the Bare caught Him by one leg and drew Him back wards down the tree. . . . It appears his Head Was In the Bares mouth at least twice—and that When the monster give the Crush that Was to mash the mans Head . . . the Head Sliped out only the teeth Cutting the Skin to the bone Where Ever the [bear] tuched it—so that the Skin of the Head was Cut from about the Ears to the top in Several derections—all of Which Wounds Ware Sewed up as Well as Cold be don by men In our Situation Haveing no Surgen nor Surgical Instruments—the man Still Retained His Under Standing but Said I am killed . . . I Heard my Skull Brake—" Lewis Dawson died three days later.

Now I see why teachers teach spelling and punctuation—to make stories easier to read!

page 59   **Diphtheria.** The story of how William Bent was healed of diphtheria by a famous Cheyenne medicine man the Americans called "Old Lawyer" is true.

page 60   **Owl Woman (Mis-stan-stur).** William Bent's first wife was described by Lieutenant J. W. Abert in his 1845 journal. "In the evening I got a fine sketch of 'Mis-stan'stur,' a Cheyenne . . . who has been married (to William Bent) for several years (and) has had two children. . . . Having a white man for her husband, she has not been obliged to work, therefore her hands are in all their native beauty, small, delicately formed. . . ." After Owl Woman died in childbirth, William Bent married her sister, Yellow Woman.

page 70   **Flute.** A young Cheyenne man circled outside the lodge of the girl of his dreams, playing songs on a flute he had made. If the girl was interested, she would briefly slip outside, and the courtship would begin.

page 71   **Eagle feathers** were a valuable trade item among the Native American plains people. Two dozen feathers could be traded for a pony.

page 74   **The battle between Pawnee and Cheyenne** was a skirmish that actually took place on an island in the Arkansas River. The Cheyenne built a grass fire to smoke out their enemies, but the smoke hid the Pawnee instead. Chief Whirlwind was hit in the jaw by a bullet that knocked out half his teeth. William Bent witnessed the battle and is reported to have told the Cheyenne chiefs to stop the nonsense before someone was killed. Nevertheless, a young Pawnee brave died before the battle fizzled out and the Cheyenne moved up the Arkansas toward Bent's Fort. The true story of this battle and death of the young Pawnee brave is the basis for the battle and death of the Pawnee brave in this story.

page 80   **Count coup.** A daring feat of bravery performed by a brave, ranging from capturing a horse to killing an enemy. Touching an enemy without killing him was considered the bravest "coup."

page 82   **Buffalo.** The Cheyenne used all parts of the buffalo: the stomach for holding and heating liquids such as soup; bones for spoons and other utensils; hide for clothing and shelter; meat for eating raw, cooked, dried into jerky, or pounded into pemmican; and even the hair for braiding into strong rope.

page 88   **Big Timbers.** A favorite camping area that stretched for forty-five miles along the Santa Fe Trail beside the Arkansas River near the present town of Lamar, Colorado. It was known for its enormous cottonwood trees, one of which grew to sixteen feet in circumference. (Just how big is that? Measure out sixteen feet of string and put it in a circle on the floor. That's a pretty big tree, isn't it?)

page 92   **Colonel Charles Alexander Warfield.** Warfield schemed to form and lead an expedition of volunteers to overthrow the government in the northern Mexican provinces and win the allegiance of the citizens for Texas. He proposed to accomplish his aim by robbing Mexican wagon trains and splitting the booty

with the government of the Independent
Republic of Texas. Recruits from Missouri who
robbed and murdered Don Antonio Chávez
forgot about splitting the booty. They were
nothing more than greedy highway robbers.

page 96   **Pro-slavery.** Admitting new states into the
United States strengthened or weakened the
balance of power for and against slavery.
Southern states favored admitting Texas into
the Union as a pro-slavery state.

page 97   **Pawnee Rock.** A large, isolated rise topped
with rock near the present town of Larned,
Kansas, a lookout point where daring travelers
scratched names into rocks in spite of the
danger of attack by plains tribes. Many
unmarked graves surround the site.

page 114   **Sign language.** People who spoke different
languages commonly communicated with
signs, but death could result from
misinterpreted signals. The American signal
for "get away" was the Cheyenne sign for
"hurry, come." In 1847, the kindhearted, well-
loved old Cheyenne Chief Cinemo, known by
Americans as "Old Tobacco," was killed by a
teamster with a U.S. government wagon train
as he peacefully approached to ask for
tobacco—possibly as a result of a
misunderstood hand signal. With his dying
breath, Chief Cinemo told the Cheyenne not
to seek revenge but to maintain peace. In this
story, Chief Cinemo's tragic story is the source

of the misunderstood signal between Zar and Wounded Brave.

page 123 **Manifest Destiny.** A phrase in a newspaper article written by John O'Sullivan claiming that United States expansion into new territories was inevitable and divinely ordained (see John O'Sullivan).

page 123 **Owl Creek** later became known as Chávez Creek in honor of the murdered trader. Now the creek is called "Jarvis Creek." (Can you guess why?) Today, people still search the banks of Jarvis Creek for remnants of Don Antonio's stolen gold.

page 133 **Shrink-wrapped gold bullion.** Although it is true that people protected gold bullion by wrapping it in wet leather that would shrink to fit, we know from recorded history that Don Antonio's gold was actually in the form of gold dust and gold coins.

page 154 **Pawnee village.** Descriptions of crops and the detail of the woven pumpkin-skin mat are taken from interviews with elderly Pawnee collected in the mid-1930s. Descriptions of the bear claw necklace and the grizzly robe come from early photographs. Descriptions of the mound houses and tools are based on sketches, some by early European-American explorers, and some more modern interpretations of Pawnee life drawn in the mid-1800s.

page 182 **John O'Sullivan.** A writer for the *United States Magazine and Democratic Review,* well aware of an ill-fated Texan invasion of Mexico.

After the bungling Texans wandered around lost in the desert until nearly dead, they were captured. Mexican troops declared a great victory and forced their prisoners to march to Mexico City to a varmint-infested jail. Another writer, newspaperman George Kendall, was among those arrested. After Kendall's release, his scathing reports inflamed American passions against Mexico. Coupled with American enthusiasm for expansion, Kendall's reports undoubtedly influenced John O'Sullivan, who coined the term *Manifest Destiny* in an article. The phrase caught on immediately with an American public eager to believe in their divine right to western lands regardless of current inhabitants.

Glossary

A*d*obe	A mixture of clay, water, and a binder such as straw, poured into molds and sun dried to make bricks.
Bo*n*ita	Spanish for "pretty."
Cami*n*emos	Spanish for "Let's walk," "Let's go," or "Let's get going."
Ca*s*ita	Spanish for "little house."
Chi*v*ita	Spanish for "little goat"; the name of Julio's dog.
Co*m*ál	A flat metal cooking pan.
Dios	Spanish for "God."
E-peva’e	Cheyenne for "Thank you."
Freebooter	A person who robs; a pirate on land or sea.
*Gra*cias	Spanish for "thank you."
*Háh*nama	Cheyenne for "bear."
*H*ola	Spanish for "hi" or "hello."
*J*oven	Spanish for "young man."
Kits ka	Pawnee name for the Arkansas River.
Los Pere*z*osos	Spanish for "the lazy ones."
*Mon*te	A Mexican card game.
Néške’e	Cheyenne for "Grandmother."
O*v*ejas	Spanish for "sheep."
Panta*l*o*n*es	Spanish for "pants" or "trousers."
Sa*r*a*p*e	An open-sided jacket.
Sternwheeler	A riverboat with paddles in the rear.
Teradeda	Pawnee for "enemy."
Tse-tsėhésė	Cheyenne for "Cheyenne" meaning "our people" or "we who are alike."

Tienes hambre?	Spanish for "Do you have hunger?" or "Are you hungry?"
Vamos	Spanish for "Let's go."
Ven	Spanish for "Come here!"
Yucca	A tall plant with spiked leaves that grow from a center root. Yucca root was used as soap by Native Americans.